DELBERT'S WEIR

By Carmen Peone

ISBN-13:978-1519414953
ISBN-10:1519414951

This novel is a work of fiction. Names, descriptions, entities, and incidents included in the story are products of the author's imagination. Any resemblance to actual persons, events, and entities is entirely coincidental.

Cover design and formatting by Rossano Designs

Young Adult Books
by Carmen Peone

Change of Heart
Heart of Courage
Heart of Passion

DEDICATION

To my parents, Lew and Jean Sutton,
who gave me a love for the outdoors.

ACKNOWLEDGEMENTS

I would like to thank the following folks for helping Delbert's Weir come alive. These professionals freely shared advice and wisdom with me about tribal ways of fishing, red band trout and other fish, rocks and minerals and trapping and snaring techniques to make Delbert's Weir as authentic to the Colville Tribe and tribal setting up Hall Creek as can be. Thank you Ricky Desautel for sharing traditional trapping and snaring techniques with me, Dr. Randy Sandaine N.D. for assistance with native plants and wasps and reactions to them, Marshall Peone for his geological knowledge with rocks and minerals, Joe Peone for his knowledge of fishing on the Colville Confederated Reservation, Sheri Sears for hooking me up with the red band trout photos and information, and finally Abe Best lll and Ted Cohen for your time teaching me about the importance of traditional Native American fishing and the use of the fence style weir on the Okanogan River.

Northeast
Washington Territory

CHAPTER 1

July, 15 1870
Day One

Delbert stood at the edge of the Sinyekst village and tossed a rock back and forth in his hands. He glared at Pekam as fear and frustration curled in his gut. The rock landed in one hand, then was flung to the other. He'd waited twelve months for this adventure and now it slid to a halt. Promises broken. Hope shattered.

He stopped lobbing the rock and watched the Indian village wake up. Why was this happening to him? What now? He watched little boys pretend to hunt as they waved branches and sticks at one another as though they were spears and knifes. Little girls held faceless dolls dressed in buckskin while they sat near their mothers who cooked over open fires and visited. Native words filled his ears. Some he recognized, most he didn't. He tried to decide how to persuade Pekam to guide this outing. Angry thoughts blocked his mind as frustration percolated inside. He turned his attention back to Pekam, a look of regret on his face.

"What do you mean you're *not* comin'?" Delbert Gardner's words sounded as angry as vibrating rattles on a tip of a rattlesnake. Color drained from his face as he stared at Pekam, his longtime Sinyekst friend. *I can't do this myself. I'm sure we'll starve, but I'm not gonna turn back like a coward.*

He tried to stand rigid but his knees wobbled. Anger welled up in is gut. He felt his face redden as deep as the scraggly hair on top his head, and looked straight at the twenty-eight-year-old man.

Pekam grinned back. "You'll be fine. You and the other boys will only be gone a few days."

"No! I won't. You're the one whose name means bobcat and for a reason. I don't have many survival skills. You were gonna teach me, us, remember? I'm sixteen now…" Delbert scrunched his face and kicked the ground with the toe of his dusty cowboy boot.

Delbert's skin crawled as he watched Pekam lean against the pole horse corral, arms folded. He stood relaxed. Patient. Delbert tapped his foot. Let his eyes dart from his friend, to the trees, and back again.

Delbert breathed slow and controlled. He studied Pekam's six-foot, tule-pit house and how it differed from his small but cozy log cabin. Smoke rolled out of the circular home made of tightly woven tule-reed mats arranged over a wooden frame. His own home was made on top of the earth, from logs, and was chinked with mud.

"You understand my horse took a hard tumble down the side of that mountain." Pekam pointed to the hill behind Delbert. His black and white Paint horse stood in the corral, leg cocked, head down. "He's still limping and I need to stay here with him. We have races coming up in ten days, and we're counting on a sale the next day. He's favored to win."

"Yeah, I do understand. But I'm not sure." Delbert shuddered. He glanced around and searched for answers amongst the fir trees, hoped the breeze would whisper some words of encouragement. He watched Pekam out of the corner of his eyes. He appeared confident in buckskin pants and shirt, long braids, and beaded moccasins.

"I know you were counting on me, but this colt's been faithful, and I need to show him the same amount of respect in return. This is how we live, Delbert. Just like your pa ranches, we raise, train, and race horses."

Delbert toed the dirt. "I know, but still. I wish you were comin'. We've planned this for a year now. You and Pa agreed we could do this once I turned sixteen. Three days is all this is supposed to take."

Pekam ruffled Delbert's hair. "I realize that. I'm sorry. Besides, I'll give you detailed directions that will take you right to camp, and we can discuss catching critters before you, Jed, and Ross head out on this journey. You won't be alone. I won't leave your quiver empty," Pekam teased as he nodded at the two boys nearby.

"I hate when you say that."

Pekam jogged toward his tule-mat dwelling. Waist-long braids jigged behind him. He glanced back over his shoulder. "Forgot some herbs. Be right back."

The pit in Delbert's stomach burned as hot as a cowboy's branding fire. He glanced around the quiet, empty village. Most of Pekam's people were gone fishing for salmon up north at Kettle Falls this time of year. Each year they loaded horses, travois, and canoes and made the thirty-five mile trek to catch and dry the fish—their main staple.

Delbert felt isolated in the mountains filled with pine, larch, and fir trees that surrounded the area. *I'm no good at this. I can't survive. What am I doin'? We should go back. I'm not my pa. He can do anything.* He dropped his face into his trembling hands.

"What're you mumbling 'bout?" Jed asked.

Delbert lifted his gaze and studied his two friends. Jed reminded him of a young larch tree, his thin legs took long strides. His short, sandy-brown hair spread out made him look like a drenched porcupine. The top of Ross's head came up to the bottom of Jed's chin. Ross's dark brown eyes matched his hair color and he wore a serious look. His muscles bulged.

"You're not gonna turn tail and back out, are ya?" Ross glared at his friend.

Delbert glanced from Jed to Ross and gave them a crooked grin. "No, well, I…maybe. We don't know enough to survive by ourselves. Pekam was supposed to teach me—us, his ways." His gaze dropped to the dirt.

"What do you mean, you don't know?" Ross said. "Your pa's an expert. He traps, hunts, herds cows and does it all on one good leg. For the love of coyote bait, we're sixteen." He looked at Jed. "Well, almost. We're men. We can do this. Don't need no help. At least I don't."

Jed snorted. "Where've you been all these years? I know we all don't get to see much of each other with Ross livin' down Lincoln and me over the hill from you, but I figured you knew all this."

Delbert looked away.

4

Ross scrunched his face. "You spend too much time with your books and rocks. Heck, all ya do is daydream with your ma in front of a cozy fire. You might as well wear an apron."

"It's not like I don't know anything." Delbert clenched his jaw. "I've trapped with my pa, and, yes, I know how to shoot a rifle. I have more hair under my hat than ya think," his voice softened, "but you're right. I rather read my books."

Jed looked down. "No one said you was ignorant. We thought ya knew more, is all."

"Have you ever bagged a deer, grouse, anything?" Ross asked.

Delbert shifted his weight before shaking his head.

"Nothing?" Ross screeched.

"Nothing. I admit it. I'm worthless," Delbert snapped back.

"You're not worthless," Jed said. "I still wanna go. We can do this. Between the three of us I 'spect we can figure it out."

"Yeah, it's not that tough. We gotta go." Ross's eyes sparkled. "We'll have an adventure: hunt, fish, camp and all under the stars. I feel like I can't sharpen my knife fast enough."

"Pekam told me he would teach us some things before we headed out. So let's spend the night here and leave in the morning," Delbert suggested.

"Okay, after we eat breakfast, right? Your Aunt Spupaleena's cookin' alone is worth the wait, or so I hear," Jed said as he punched Delbert in the arm.

Delbert swallowed hard and wiped the sweat from

5

his eyes. The heat spiked as the afternoon sun hung high in the sky, but the breeze and scent of cool water wafting off the meandering Columbia River called to Delbert and his friends, inviting them to splash in its coolness.

Delbert studied the river and noticed all the rock islands he hadn't paid much attention to in the past. The river rippled around the solid masses and pooled between them, creating only a couple safe places to cross. A gentle but swift flow swept the water downriver.

"Let's go for a quick swim before we meet up with Pekam." Ross scrunched his face at Delbert's hair as it spiked as straight as a patch of new spring grass.

Delbert lifted his chin toward the river. "You guys go. I'll be right behind ya. I wanna check on his colt."

The wiry boys sprinted toward the river. "Don't take too long," Jed shouted back over his shoulder.

Delbert waved them off with a sense of relief and took time to think their adventure through. He watched his pals head to the river. Cracks of doubt tugged at his heart. *Can I pull this off? Will Jed and Ross be much help?* He rubbed the back of his neck as the two disappeared down the hill to the beach.

He slipped behind Pekam and watched him wash and place herbs on the colt's legs. The colt stood quiet as Pekam wrapped each leg with strips of buckskin. The horse remained quiet while he was rubbed down with a poultice made of inner fibers of willow bark and honeysuckle root.

"How'd you get him to stand that way?"

Pekam jerked around as the horse shuffled sideways. "Hey, what are you doing? I thought you would be at the river with Jed and Ross."

6

"I...I..."

"You what?"

Delbert shrugged. "I wanted to watch you doctor your horse. That's all."

The startled look on Pekam's face turned soft. "I know. Sorry." He relaxed his stance. "You startled me–us. Here, you want to help?" He reached for some buckskin strips and tossed them to Delbert.

Delbert caught them with one hand. "Sure."

They worked in the stillness of the morning. No words spoken between them.

Later, Pekam asked, "Delbert, what are you so afraid of out there?"

The searing fire in Delbert's stomach burned hotter. "I'm not sure." He quit wrapping a hind leg and thought for a moment.

Pekam's horse lowered his head and blinked as silence lingered.

"I've watched you with your Pa," Pekam said. "You have plenty of skills. I'm not sure about the other two, but I know you do. Why don't you believe that?"

A mix of irritation and embarrassment seared his nerves. He squeezed the bandage, wanting to drop it and run off, but stroked the horse's leg and continued to wrap the wound instead.

"You don't have to be a skilled trapper or hunter to get the job done." Pekam peered at Delbert.

"Don't I?" He sighed. "You know I prefer to study geology with my ma and read books about, well, anything to do with rocks, minerals, and rock formations. It's something we share. Minerals are more important than folks realize." Delbert finished wrapping the leg and checked his work. "That part of the Lord's creation is what sparks a fire inside me."

The colt lifted his leg to get a feel for the wrap. He shook it a couple times, looked back, and snorted.

Pekam tied a thin strip of buckskin around the front leg to hold the wrap tight. He stretched his long, lean muscles and ran his hand down the Paint's withers. His soft facial features made him look younger than he was.

Delbert thought of how Pekam and his sister, Spupaleena, had spent the past twelve years raising a large herd of Paint horses. They had become some of the toughest and fastest racers in the territory. "Look at what you and Aunt Spupaleena built. Her dream came true. With your help. What I see is hard work and persistence has made your dream come alive. I want mine to happen. Just like yours did. Even if Pa thinks I'm soft."

Pekam's coffee-colored eyes narrowed as he looked down at Delbert. "I agree that there's nothing like exploring what the Creator has laid out for us. But He also expects us to work. We have to hunt and fish for our food, make our own clothes, and care for those we love, both human and animal. And why do you think your pa doesn't support you. I know he does."

"What do you mean? I know we have to work to survive." Delbert fiddled with a strip of buckskin laying over the fence pole. "I don't think my pa supports me because he doesn't ask me to go with him anymore."

Pekam nodded and thought a minute. "Learning about what interests you is never wrong, like studying rocks and minerals, but that's *not* more important than the tasks we perform to stay alive. This country is rugged and cruel. With hard work, your quiver will remain full." Pekam rubbed his horse. "Maybe you should talk to your Pa about why he doesn't ask you to tag along?"

Delbert stroked the colt's back. "Full or empty, I'll let the Lord fill my *quiver*. And. Well. I reckon I could ask. I just figured he didn't want me with him."

"I think you might be surprised. Perhaps you and your pa need to talk this over. Anyway, grab your weapon of choice and let's get started."

"Doing what?"

Pekam groaned.

"Oh, yeah. Huntin' lessons." Delbert's expression brightened.

"Go get the boys. I think it's safest to start with one weapon. Perhaps a dull arrow. With cattail fluff on the end."

Delbert headed for the river, unsure whether to laugh or be offended.

Chapter 2

"Hey, over here. Come on!" Delbert shaded his vision from the blistering sun. He squinted his eyes and saw two gangly figures darting back and forth down the Columbia River shoreline. Their voices shrieked and bounced off the mountains from across the river. They played like little boys—Jed towered over Ross.

By the time Delbert reached his friends, he was out of breath. Sweat rolled down his face and neck. Jed and Ross covered their noses and made gagging sounds. Delbert pumped his fists.

"What's wrong with you? We're only teasing." Jed smirked at Ross.

Delbert shoved them into the river's current. They swam to shore with quick strokes and tore out after Delbert who was short and stocky, strong as an ox, but never a sprinter. He peered over his shoulder at the two wiry, waterlogged boys chasing him like a mountain lion after a deer. He tried to laugh and run at the same time, but tripped over a branch and slammed into the rock-littercd path. Jed and Ross jumped him. The three boys wrestled and cackled until their sides heaved.

"Who smells like a rotten coyote carcass now?"

Delbert punched Ross in the arm. He turned his nose to the sky and sniffed the air. "Not me, you half-decayed varmints."

Jed and Ross exchanged devious glances and grasped Delbert by the arms and ankles and hauled him to the river for an ice-cold bath.

The sun was on a downward slope when Delbert and the boys decided to make their way back to the village—dripping a trail behind them. Delbert saw Pekam and Spupaleena's attention drift his way. He heard them discussing horses.

"So this is what you have to work with, huh, Pekam?" Spupaleena flashed a teasing smirk at Delbert, reflecting spunk, as her rabbit name implied.

Delbert grunted. "We can hear you, ya know."

The boys stopped in front of the siblings.

Pekam nodded. "They worry me."

Delbert plopped his hands on his hips and shook his head as he leaned forward.

Spupaleena squealed as drops of water splashed her bare arms and face. "I can see why. Better you than me, brother."

Spupaleena snickered. "You look like a pack of squirrels that have been caught in a wet wind storm." She eyed each boy.

"Glad you're amused, Aunt Spup." Delbert swiped water off the back of his neck.

"Go change into something dry so we can get in a

little training before dinner," Pekam said.

"What's for dinner?" Delbert asked Spupaleena.

"Drown salmon and waterlogged bannock." Spupaleena said in Sinyekst.

Pekam and Spupaleena howled as they strode off.

Delbert glanced at his friends and mocked the siblings' laughter.

Once in dry clothing, the boys met Pekam at the outskirts of the village for practice. Pekam started them off pulling back arrows tipped with jagged-edged arrowheads on bows made of smooth western yew. Horsetail stem had been used to make the bows as smooth as polished rocks.

Delbert watched Ross aim, let his arrow loose, and miss the target by several inches, a leaf tacked to a tree stump by a pinch of pitch. Jed squawked and danced in circles like a chick chased by a hawk. But his turn was not much better. Ross scoffed and searched for the lost arrow. When he returned, Delbert drew back his bow and stared down the arrow toward a pinecone perched on a stump. He released his grip and the taut string snapped his forearm. The boy squealed in pain and tossed his bow to the side. He hopped up and down and held his arm to his chest.

Pekam rubbed his brow. "It can't be this tough," he mumbled.

"Come on, Delbert. My little sister can shoot better'n that," Ross teased.

Delbert's face shined pink and his lips pursed. Pekam placed a steady hand on the boy as Delbert let the air gush through his teeth.

"Okay, that's enough for now. We'll try again in a

while, perhaps knife throwing for some amusement. I'm hungry." Pekam walked Delbert back toward the village, guided by dinner's aroma wafting through the air.

Delbert took hold of the wooden bowl Spupaleena held out while she filled it full of steaming salmon, bannock, and fried cabbage Elizabeth Gardner had sent with her son. He gobbled his food and glanced at Spupaleena, begging for more. She refilled his empty bowl. Delbert walked his second helping and a leather pouch to a grassy spot behind Pekam's tule-pit home.

He slid to the ground and leaned against an old larch stump to study the cliff face pattern that overlooked the river. He marveled at God's handiwork. Thoughts of a failed journey snuck into his heart. He sighed as he picked at his salmon. *You formed the mountains by your power and armed yourself with such strength. Ya wanna share some of that strength with me?*

His appetite dissolved, so he placed the bowl on the ground. He plucked a thin pamphlet from his pouch about minerals and rock formations his ma gave him from when she was in school back east. He opened it as if the pages would crumble under his touch. He scanned each page and searched for rocks and minerals in the area. Some of them looked familiar. His fingers slid across the pages for a few moments, but his mind was elsewhere. He closed the leaflet, leaned his head against the stump and closed his eyes. Dreams of teaching geology in some fancy school back east, where his ma was from, lulled him to sleep.

"Do you think we'll be okay without Pekam?" Jed asked Ross.

"Why wouldn't we?"

"I don't know. But do ya?"

"Of course, we will. We got fish hooks and knives and the food our mas sent with us. I'm sure Spupaleena will throw in extra food, too. You can see Delbert and them are more like family than friends. We'll be spoiled for sure." Ross punched Jed. "Quit your frettin'. You sound like an old lady."

"Yeah. I reckon your right."

"I'm always right!"

A gentle breeze blanked them with warm air as water dried from their skin.

"What do you think Pekam will teach us first?" Jed asked.

"I hope knife throwing."

"That would be fun. I know I could stab me a rabbit or two as quick as the blink of an eye." Jed flicked his wrist as if throwing a knife into the clouds.

Ross laughed. "Maybe as quick as a turtle crossin' a log."

"Watch me then. I'll show you."

Ross laughed harder.

"Better than you, you yellow-bellied skunk."

Ross rolled to his side and tried to catch his breath in between spasms of laughter.

Jed stood and kicked sand on Ross.

Ross laughed so hard his anger wouldn't ignite.

Jed stomped off.

"Wait for me," Ross said.

Jed kept walking.

Later that night, Delbert and the other two followed Pekam into the woods to practice snaring small game.

"What's the best spot to place the loop?" Pekam asked.

"Close to the ground," Ross replied.

"Where tracks lead toward the water," Jed chimed in.

Delbert looked down and shrugged, his gaze glued to the shiny rock in his hand.

Pekam dropped his chin. "Delbert, for being so upset about me not leading *your* expedition, you seem pretty uninterested."

"I heard you. Where to place the snare…close to the ground…where the tracks are." He placed the rock in his pocket, held out his braided hemp rope and formed a loop. "Like this right?"

"We're not there yet." Pekam snorted. "Show me one more place where a snare should be set up."

Delbert scanned the terrain. "Over there." He pointed to a tuft of scrub brush.

Pekam pressed a finger to his temple. "No wonder your pa complains."

"You said earlier the branches need to be small." Delbert could feel his throat tighten.

"I did. But they also need to be strong enough to hold the captured animal, not break off at its first attempt to escape."

Delbert fingered the rock in his pocket. *What's the point? I'm not good enough.* He shifted his weight. "Okay. I get it."

Pekam examined his loop. "Now tie it off, and we'll go set these other traps. In the morning, before you boys head into the Hall Creek hills, we'll see if you actually nabbed anything."

Chapter 3

July 16, 1867
Day Two

Balmy morning air swirled the earth; it was warmer than usual for early July. Delbert hoped practice would go better than the day before. He roused his two sleeping pals and sprang out of Pekam's tule-pit home. A blend of smoke and food from the morning cooking fires met him. "Flapjacks!" His stomach stirred. He watched Spupaleena whip some up from the mix his mother sent with him.

Spupaleena poured batter onto a hot skillet Delbert's ma had given her. He recalled how she'd been lost and hurt so many years ago and how his pa found her. He glanced down at the snare he fingered and said, "Just like our families, entwine as strong as these three strands of hemp braided for this snare. Two families from separate worlds, woven with the Lord into one."

"That's right, Delbert," Spupaleena said. She smiled at him.

He gave her an awkward one back and thought what he'd said sounded an awful lot like a girl. He felt himself blush.

"Come on. Let's go check our snares," Ross said.

Delbert shoved the snare in his pocket and lit out after his two friends. He couldn't wait to get away from his silly words. They scurried into the woods, anxious to see what small critters they may be eating for their next meal.

Jed snagged a rabbit.

Ross captured a chipmunk.

Delbert's snare was empty. "I must be cursed," he said. The loop broken, his snare lay in the dirt. He kicked it and said through gritted teeth, "I'm a huntin' failure. And people wonder why I'm stuck on rocks." He glanced around and felt the heat of shame rise in his cheeks. His partners brought over their catches and burst into laughter. Shame danced around him and settled deep in his gut.

"What happened?" Ross asked.

"Not sure."

Jed began, "Well, your pa always told me…" Delbert gave him a look that could burn a hole through a rock cliff. "Um, anyway."

"Oh, come on Del, it's not so bad," Ross said.

Delbert followed behind his friends as they headed back to dress out their fresh meat and pack for their departure.

After Pekam trudged through four hours of instructions and helped load the packs and tie them onto the back of saddles, the boys rode out. Delbert twisted around and waved to Pekam, who stood and smiled as if betting how long the boys would last. The trio bobbed up and down on their nags, waving to the kids who followed along behind and shouted Sinyekst good-byes.

"What are they saying?" Jed asked.

"Not sure, something about ghosts and a giant bear." Delbert turned forward. "No ghosts are gonna scare me away."

"Me either. Let's go!" Ross kicked his horse into a canter.

Once out of sight, the boys reined in their mounts.

This is gonna be fun." Jed scanned the tree-filled mountains. The sun warmed his back. He mopped his forehead with his shirtsleeve and inhaled several deep breaths. "What *is* that smell?"

Delbert lifted his nose up and sniffed. "Sumac. It's sweet, exhilarating, lush sumac. I love that smell more than anything."

Ross also inhaled the aroma. "Yeah, it's okay."

Jed rode close to Ross. He attempted to push the boy off his horse. Delbert's thoughts lingered on the gray-blue hue of the rock formations to the west. Look over there, he pointed. "Looks like an old Sinyekst man. The good Lord sure has a sense of humor."

"Yeah, he does. They always look old," Jed added.

Delbert's mind wandered to images of other faces and animals he had seen in rock cliffs and formations. "Have you ever seen a cliff profile look like a girl?"

"Come to think of it, no," Jed answered.

Ross snorted. "Why you ask?"

"Well, have ya?" Delbert pointed out to the side. "Look over there. Looks like an ol' man. Never seen one look like a girl. Huh, I wonder why?"

21

"Not one that's young and not one that's old." Jed shaded his eyes with his hand. "I reckon we've never seen a girl because they're prettier than rocks."

Ross shook his head. "I reckon so."

Delbert and his two friends rode for several hours before coming up on the creek they would camp by that evening. A few more miles northwest is where they planned to pitch their tents.

"I think the horses need water," Delbert said.

"I need water, too." Jed slid off his horse, unhooked his canteen, gulped a nice long swallow, and looked the creek over. "Hey, Ross, where's a fishin' hook? I wanna try my luck." He sifted through his friend's saddlebag.

Ross glanced his way. "It should be right there. I rolled the hooks in some ol' buckskin Pekam gave me. Find it?"

"No. You sure? How many you pack?"

Delbert shook his head. *Swell job, boys. We'll starve for sure now.*

"It should be right there. I packed about ten of 'em. You need some spectacles, granny?"

Jed chuckled. "No. But if I did, I'd borrow 'em from you."

Ross picked up some pinecones and tossed them at Jed, one at a time. Delbert could feel the heat rise up his neck.

"C'mon now, stop it. I can't find nothin' in here." He slapped the saddlebag closed and the horse flinched.

"I have a notion to toss you in the creek." Ross strode over to Jed. "You're blind as an ol' mule." He unlaced the saddlebag from his saddle, dropped it on the ground and rifled through its contents.

"I know I packed 'em. Hey, Delbert, you take the hooks?"

"Nope."

"As a joke?" Jed asked.

"Nope." Delbert pulled his ragged-looking geology journal from his own saddlebag. He thumbed through the pages and stopped where black and white pictures showed different rocks and minerals that caught his eye. *I can't concentrate with these two carrying on. What idiots. How hard is it to pack a few hooks? That was their job. They need to pull their weight.*

"Delbert, this isn't funny. Where are the hooks?" Ross dug through his packs for a second time.

"Yes, it's amusing since you always pull jokes on others. But, no, I haven't seen your hooks. Haven't looked at 'em, nor touched 'em." Delbert closed his journal. "Could it be that you forgot them?"

"I know I brought 'em."

"What about that one?" Jed pointed to the saddlebag on the other side of Jed's saddle.

"Those are clothes and food. They're not in there."

"Why don't you check?" Delbert asked. His expression turned grim.

"Because I know the hooks are in this one." Ross tapped the saddlebag on the ground with the toe of his dirty, brown cowboy boot.

"You're as ornery and stubborn as your pa." Delbert stated.

"And as dumb as your uncle," Jed hollered.

Delbert roared with laughter. "Have you seen his

23

uncle? The best dressed, tallest sittin' cowboy around."

"He's not that great," Ross muttered.

Delbert's eyes grew round. "Jack Dalley's the greatest cowboy…horse trainer…cow puncher…business man in the territory. Only a fool is blind to that!"

Ross sifted through the other saddlebag. Sweat rolled down the side of his face and stained his buckskin pack. He mopped his forehead with his sleeve and untied the saddlebag, pouring its contents in the dirt. He toed around, hoping to uncover something to save face. "They're not in here either."

"Those clothes were clean," Jed commented.

Ross glared at him.

"It's no big deal. We can whittle some spears with my knife"—Jed pulled a three inch bladed knife out of its sheath that was hooked to his belt—"besides, we've got the snares. We can set 'em up tonight once we get to camp." He slid the knife back into the sheath and announced, "I'm hungry."

Delbert nodded. "Yeah. Me, too. Where's the meat you two snared this morning?"

Ross looked at Jed. Jed shrugged.

"You two forgot the meat?"

Ross shoved his clothes back in the saddlebag, debris and all.

"We can get more meat. That was easy," Jed said.

Delbert found some dried salmon and chewed on it as he glared at his friends. When finished, he climbed into the saddle and followed the river as it wound northwest.

Delbert and his friends hit the campsite as the sun angled down. A small meadow carpeted with lush, thick grass spread before them—larch, fir, and pine encircled the camp spot. Cottonwood stood before him with familiarity. Hall Creek roared with frigid run-off from winter snow packs.

Delbert inhaled a deep breath. "I can taste the fish already." He watched the water roll down the creek. The feel of its rhythm swept down his arms.

"Wahoo!" Ross leaped off his horse and ran to the creek. He kneeled down and filled his cupped hands with the stream's current and splashed his face.

Jed followed.

Delbert eased off his saddle and placed it in the grass. He came around and put his hand on his horse's neck. "I can get a lot of reading done here." He looked forward to learning about new geological discoveries. "Someday I'll write some articles. I'll teach and share my findings with students." He stared into glistening rays of the sun as his excitement soared, thinking about the stories his mother shared with him from her time as a child growing up and getting her schooling in a small, one room school house.

"C'mon, Delbert," Jed hollered from the creek.

"I'll be there in a minute. Gonna picket the horses." Delbert kicked a branch out of the way. "Someone has to."

"Aw, just drop the reins, they're not goin' nowhere," Ross hollered.

Delbert grunted. After he tied the last horse to the picket line and made sure the cinches were loose, he sank down to the grass near the creek, leaned against a boulder. He pulled out his geological journal and thumbed through the pages. He wanted to study minerals before his buddies tugged him into the water.

Ross stepped toward Delbert and flicked water in his face. "What're you reading there?" he asked.

Jed said, "Probably something about rocks and sentimentals."

"*Sentimentals*? Do you even know what that means?" Delbert chuckled.

"Yeah, rocks and stuff."

Ross pushed Jed. "No, dummy. The proper term is *sediments*."

Jed flicked water on Ross.

A water fight broke out between the two and splashed onto Delbert. He tossed his journal aside and plunged toward his pals.

CHAPTER 4

The boys sprawled on the soft, green grass a few feet away from the creek. Delbert thought about his next move as he listened to the water tumble over rocks. He studied damp britches and shirts that hung on branches of scrub brush. *This is gonna be a great adventure.*

"What should we do now?" Delbert asked.

"I think it's time to eat. My gut's growlin'." Ross glanced around at his pals. "It won't be long till nightfall."

"What'd'ya have in mind? You forgot the fishing hooks and your morning catch," Delbert said.

"I'll catch 'em with my bare hands." Jed stretched his arms and clenched his fists as he gazed toward the summer skyline.

Ross laughed. "I'd like to see that." He eyeballed the creek.

Delbert rolled onto his stomach. "Pekam showed me how to make a fish trap when I was about eight. We could try that."

"Maybe that way *you* could actually catch something." Ross slapped his leg in a fit of laughter.

Delbert threw a rock and missed Ross's head by

inches.

"Hey, what in the blazes are you doin'? I'm just joshin'."

"I'm not," Delbert barked.

Jed stepped between the two. "How do we build this trap? What do we need first?"

A vein on Ross's neck protruded as he waited for Delbert to answer Jed.

Delbert let out a captive breath. "We need sticks." His focus remained on Ross.

"Okay. What kind?" Jed combed his hair with his fingers.

Delbert shifted his attention to Jed. "What do you mean 'what kind'? Sticks are sticks."

"Fresh? Pine? Larch?" Jed gave Delbert a matter-of-fact look.

"You two 'bout done dancin' over the type of wood we need for this thing? Does it matter? As long as it's not dead and rotted," Ross said.

Delbert shrugged. "Come on. Let's get some."

"How're you gonna make it in that fancy school you wanna go to if you can't even tell us which kinda wood to gather?" Jed asked.

"I'm not going to school for wood. I'm going for rocks, remember? Rocks." Delbert pushed to his feet and wiped grass off his pants.

"Well, rocks live with wood. Don't you need to know them both?"

Delbert shook his head. "How you'll ever survive in this land, I'll never know."

"What?" The corners of Jed's mouth formed a thin

line.

"Nothin'." Delbert waved him away. "Let's find sticks about two-feet long. About the length of your two big toes, Jed." He smiled.

Jed pushed Delbert as he guffawed.

Delbert and the boys rummaged the rocky hills for an hour until they had armfuls of sticks and fallen logs. They made their way back to camp and formed two separate piles, one with sticks for the traps, and the other for a roaring fire to roast armloads of fish. Or so Delbert hoped.

Ross glanced up. "Hey, look at those black, storm clouds rolling our way. We should have a bite to eat before making traps. It won't hurt to get a fire goin' now."

Delbert looked up. "Jed, you wanna start the fire? I'll start the traps. Ross–"

"I'll go and get some herbs and berries for dinner. There's gotta be edible roots around here somewhere. Your ma showed me some stuff while you and your pa were packing. She said you know what to look for, but I want a chance to find 'em myself." Ross walked off.

"I reckon you will." Delbert figured if he was alone, he could build the trap and search for rocks more efficiently than if he had his two friends in tow, especially Ross. "Sidewinder."

"I'll stick close and search for old pine needles, dry grass, and dry black moss to ignite the flint sparks." Jed motioned to the horses. "A little horsehair would sure do, too. Reckon I can rustle up both."

The boys scattered in different directions.

Delbert jabbed sticks upright into the sand, one at a time. He started from the bank and finished in the water.

He formed a heart-type shape at the top, leaving a small space for the fish to enter and not escape. After checking his work, he said, "Haven't made one of these in a long time. Glad it's easy." He studied the ground, littered with pinecones, leaves, weeds, and wildflowers. "What's hard is catching the bait."

Once finished, he admired his trap. A smile spread over his face and he swelled with a sense of accomplishment. The sticks aligned side by side just as Pekam had shown him a few years back. He wished his Sinyekst uncle was there, especially since he's of the Bull Trout people. More than likely, trout would swim into the traps. "How fitting. Yep, he'd be proud."

"What's fittin'?" Jed walked up behind his friend. "Talking to yourself again?"

"Look." Delbert pointed to his fish trap.

"Wow, this's fine work." Jed inspected the mismatched branches that stood guard like wooden soldiers. "I can already taste the fish."

"Me, too."

"What're you two gawkin' at?" A smirk creased Ross's face as he held up bulging buckskin pouches.

"Delbert's fish trap."

Ross dropped his pouches in the grass and walked to the shoreline. "You built this?" He knelt closer to the trap. He scanned the sticks that poked up from the shallow water. "I can't believe you did this. I'm not trying to be funny. This is great, Del. Can't wait to eat some fish."

Delbert beamed as confidence bubbled inside of him. "Me, either. What'd you get?" He jerked his head toward Ross's pouches lying on the grass.

Ross's eyes flashed with excitement. "I did it. I found all the plants and roots your ma showed me. I couldn't believe it. She told me where they might be, according to what Spupaleena and that old grumpy healer woman taught her."

Jed and Delbert flashed each other a surprised look and said in unison, "Simillkameen."

"That's her, all right. What does Simillkameen mean anyway?" Ross asked.

Delbert snorted. "It means swan. Not sure why she was given that name, she's far from long and graceful. The one time that old woman laughed is when my Uncle Pekam whipped all the men in one of the biggest horse races ever. He was younger than us then." He motioned to Ross with a lopsided smile on his face. "Pekam sure was fast."

"I remember hearing stories about that." Ross said. "Uncle Jack loves to tell 'em."

"Yeah, I barely remember being there. I was real little. My Aunt Spupaleena had to pull out when her horse came up lame. She had to walk him all the way back to where they started."

"What happened?" Jed leaned forward.

"A branch got stuck in the horse's leg as she was jumpin' over a tree fell by a wind storm. It was something that hardly ever happens."

"That'd be a hoot. I mean racin'." Jed paused. "Think she'd let me ride one of her race horses sometime? Aren't her horses faster than her brother's horses?"

Delbert shoved him sideways. "Are ya kiddin'? No one gets to ride 'em. Well, maybe Pekam, but that's all. In fact, no one gets to even touch 'em."

31

"Except my uncle," Ross chimed in.

Delbert nodded. "I did get to rub down one of Aunt Spupaleena's colts last year. He's not as fast or strong as the others. Not yet anyhow. Still has growin' to do. But you're right, no one else even gets to look their way."

"It was a good thought anyhow," Jed said.

Ross glanced over his shoulder. "How's that fire comin'?"

They could see a thin layer of smoke rising. "I best check on it." Jed stoked the orange embers.

Delbert glanced at his trap in the dim light of dusk one last time, then he and Ross sat around the roaring fire. He imagined roasting fish. Even smelled them. His stomach gurgled.

Black storm clouds continued to roll against the darkening horizon. A raindrop tapped the end of Delbert's nose. He wiped it away with his shirtsleeve and glanced up. "We need to pay attention to those clouds fillin' the sky."

"I can't believe this storm came up on us this quick. Let's get some shelter built." Ross rose.

Delbert scrambled about and erected canvas tents. He and Ross cut fir bows for bedding and placed them inside. Delbert glanced over at Jed and watched him restack firewood.

"I'm gonna go set a couple of snares in case it starts pourin'. Don't wanna get caught in the storm," Ross said.

"Swell idea, I'll come with you." Jed scooped up a bundle of thick, ragged-looking hemp.

"You gonna use that?" Delbert eyeballed the rolled up mess.

"What else? It may look bad, but it works. My pa gave it to me before we left. He uses it all the time."

Ross chuckled. "Come on." Jed set a three-foot stick on the fire. Once the flames took hold, he followed.

"I'll check my fish trap. Fish'll be fryin' when you boys return." Delbert stood with certainty, his spine long and straight.

He jogged to the creek, dropped to his knees, and with intent scanned the shallow water. His brow furrowed. *No fish tonight.*

Jed and Ross stopped in front of small tracks.

Jed knelt and traced the foot prints with a finger. "What do ya think? Rabbit? Squirrel?"

"Squirrel."

Jed chuckled. "I bet you can't even tell the difference between a squirrel and chipmunk track. I bet there isn't even a difference."

"It's gotta be a squirrel. Chipmunks are so light they rarely leave a visible print."

"How'd you learn that?"

"My Pa. We eat a lot of squirrel. It's a little stringy, but mighty tasty."

Jed stood, mouth open. "Can't imagine there's much meat."

"Not much at all."

Ross rubbed his head. "Let's keep looking. I bet we'll come on a rabbit trail soon enough. Our fresh meat with

Delbert's fish will be a fine supper."

"Fine with me," Jed agreed.

The boys walked on. They kept close to the water.

CHAPTER 5

"I'll be." Delbert dunked his hands into the creek and swished them around. *Are my eyes playing tricks on me? Maybe the local fish camouflage themselves against rocks and sticks like some lizards and bugs do in the desert.*

He sat back on his heels and scrutinized the trap. *No holes between the sticks.* He scanned the beach for any sign of flopping fish or even a dead, stinky one. A couple of frogs the size of a coin hopped along. Broken off twigs and dead leaves littered the sand. He sat still a moment and racked his brain for answers. "Bait." He slammed the palm of his hand against his forehead. "I'm so stupid. I can't believe I forgot the bait. I'm horrible at this. Can't even complete a simple task." He swallowed hard, fought off the lump in his throat, and looked upward in hopes of a written answer amongst the clouds.

Delbert searched for a solid stick to hold the bait. He spotted one a few feet away and snatched it up like a trophy. He dragged a knife out of its sheath that hung from his belt and held the smooth, cedar handle. He sliced a few inches down the middle of the stick with deft hands.

"All I need now are crickets." He looked around and

saw none. Bugs covered the ground. Toads squabbled in the distance. But no crickets. He sank to his knees and combed through grass and pine needles with his fingers. He closed his eye lids and thought hard. Images of his pa's fingers picking at the rich dirt flashed in his mind. His lids flung opened and he began to dig.

"Pa used worms to fish with, so worms it is." The dirt was cold and rocky and the hole was half inch deep.

He sprang to his feet, ran to his pack, and pulled out a small shovel he'd planned to dig through the river bed and investigate local sediments. That would be later. He found wet dirt and dug with the shovel a few inches. Rocks and grass roots made digging tough, so he used his foot as leverage. Chunks of black earth ripped loose and soon out popped the end of a fat worm. A sense of reprieve washed over him as confidence began to bubble up—as little as it was.

Delbert walked back to the shore, his step a bit lighter. He pushed the middle of the worm into the slit of the stick, making sure it wouldn't tear, then held the stick in front of him. He took a minute to admire his work before he jabbed the stick, worm side down, into the bottom of the creek. The stick stood as if proud in the middle of the trap. Or did that pride belong to Delbert?

The worm wiggled in the slit.

Delbert hiked back to the tent and stoked the near dead fire. He tossed the last of the kindling on and searched for more downed logs. His stomach grumbled. "When did I eat last?' Not remembering, he loaded his arms with scraps of wood and headed back. As he walked, he made mental notes to scope out some sediments from the creek bed that evening. He knew some old-timers said this area was packed with volcanic rock in the mountains closer to the Columbia River. "I sure wanna check them parts out."

He knew Pekam's people used that type of rock in their sweat lodges to hold in heat. A little water poured on top produced steam that cleansed the body from whatever ailed them. Pureness washed over them like a stringent shower.

A smile formed on his face as he remembered the time he'd snuck in with some elders. His parents visited with Pekam's family and they were having a good laugh over something he cared nothing about—he was bored and curious. He'd snuck over to the sweat lodge, stripped down to his shorts, and crawled under the buckskin door. It didn't take long for a dizzy feeling to overcome him and he felt the gnarled fingers of an elder drag his eight-year-old self out before he fainted. He'd never live that down. That being the first and last time he ever stepped foot into a death trap like that.

By the time Delbert reached camp, the rain was more of a drizzle and the fire a soggy mess. He dumped his armful of wood inside the canvas tent to keep dry and looked around for sign of Jed or Ross. He saw none and rummaged through the packs for food and found a half loaf of bread and some dried apples. He tore off a hunk of bread and shoved it in his mouth. Then popped in a couple pieces of apple and chewed. Every slim piece was savored. Once the last bite was down, he scavenged the packs for more, but came up empty.

Delbert shrugged on his wool jacket and marched to his trap, confident there would be several fish circling the bait inside. But his heart sank. The creek's swollen current had washed most of the sticks downriver. Even the baited stick was gone.

He picked up several stones, tossed them into the creek, and yelled out his frustration. Tears welled in his eyes and heat ran up his neck, so he splashed water on his face and sat in the grass. *How dumb and worthless can I be?* He let raindrops muffle the words, but his soul knew the sound and its meaning. His gut clenched, and he felt bile rise and burn his throat. He sat for a while longer before trekking back to the waterlogged fire pit.

"Where are you good-for-nothing…?" He searched camp for the others, but only saw empty tents and wet logs. "I'm tired of being the responsible one. I wish you'd carry your weight for once," he hollered. Delbert glanced at the horses. They stopped eating and grass stuck out of their mouths as they ogled him. "What are you looking at?" He shook his head.

Delbert combed his fingers through greasy hair. He grabbed a buckskin pouch from his tent and went in search of dry tinder. "Where am I going to find any? God, I sure could use some direction. A miracle or two can't hurt. I'm tired of this. I'm ready to go back"— Delbert tripped over a pile of pinecones, rolled over, and shot back up—"stinking cones!" He kicked the ground and punched a tree. Pain burst in his knuckles. He wiped blood on his pants, kicked the air, cursed some more, and headed back down the trail. East.

The sharp clip of his legs resembled an angry rooster. He walked and thought about volcanic rocks and possible sediments hidden in the creek bed. He scanned the area for a rock face with an overhang that would provide dry wood. It didn't take long to spot one several yards to his right. The cliff was almost hidden by storm clouds and fir trees.

He hustled under the rock that jutted out to get a break from the drizzle. Wet hair stuck to his face and droplets ran down his neck. His soaked shirt clung to his skin. He hated the feel of wet, sticky broadcloth. Water sprayed the rock wall as he shook his head. He glanced around the overhang. Not much to see. Then looked underneath trees mere feet away and spied long strands of black moss hanging off tree boughs.

Long branches shielded the moss from the storm like a duck protecting its young. He knew he couldn't reach the strands, not even if he stood on a stump. He spotted a stick that would reach, grabbed it and stretched up, snagging the moss on its tip. As he gathered moss he heard distant laughter. *The boys. They're back.* Delbert stuffed more moss into the pouch.

He looked up and caught a glimpse of his partners. He hollered and waved them over. They waved back and trotted in his direction, all smiles. He hoped they had at least snared a rabbit. He could feel the soft fur. Taste the juicy meat. Yet he dreaded having to admit his defeat with the fish trap. A swarm of emotions swirled inside and lodged in his throat.

"You get anything?" Delbert croaked.

"Nope. You?" Ross asked.

Delbert heaved a sigh and his shoulders fell forward. "No. The rain must have sped up the current"— he mopped his face with his jacket sleeve, flinching at the scratchy wool—"most of the sticks floated downstream."

"Well, what're you doing out here?" Jed pointed to the pack.

"Our fire pit's drenched. I was getting dry tinder. We need to get a fire going and dry out our clothes. Possibly even our blankets." Delbert shielded the rain with his hand as he peeked up at the gray sky. "Don't think this'll let up anytime soon."

Jed blinked away drops of water pecking at his eyes. "I agree. Let's get outta here."

Delbert and the boys trudged back to camp. Delbert checked on the horses, and Ross followed him. They found them with heads crammed against the tree trunks, using branches for shelter.

"Fine idea," Ross admitted to Delbert. "Hey, let's put the fire under a tree for cover, just like the horses."

Delbert nodded. "Worth a try." He retrieved a shovel leaning against a tree, dug a new pit, and piled the rocks back around the pit.

Jed spread moss out of Delbert's pack and added twigs.

Delbert struck a piece of flint with the edge of a sharp rock and sparks began to fly.

After two tries the moss lit and soon a fire blazed.

Jed added twigs and larger sticks from Delbert's tent until the fire roared enough to add larger pieces of wood.

Ross dug through his pack and found a few scraps of dried meat and brought them to the fire. He held out the morsels. Delbert eyed the meat. He eyed Ross. Then added the rest of the bread and apples to the skimpy meal. He shrugged his shoulders and said, "I guess this'll haveta do."

Jed tossed a small sack of dried huckleberries and salmon into the mix.

Ross opened the sack and jerked his head up toward Jed. "Where'd you get this?"

Jed gave him a small smile. "Spupaleena. I forgot I had it."

"When did she give it to you?" Delbert asked.

Jed cleared his throat. "Before we left."

Delbert rubbed his hands together. "Well then, boys, let's eat!"

Jed gave a quick prayer of thanks and Delbert gorged what little was in front of him while telling stories of his failed excursions. Jed and Ross shared their broken rope tale but showed off a handful of mint leaves they discovered.

"Our next meal will be fresh meat and fish with a pinch of flavoring," Ross said as he held up the mint leaves.

Delbert spoke of the missing bait and added, voice cracked, "I've got to get worms and crickets and test them to see which one works the best." He watched his partners. Their horseplay reminded him of his earlier declaration—because they're unfocused, I have to do it all. *Better get that bait myself!*

Delbert pulled his thoughts back to Ross and Jed. He laughed and joked with them, trying not to show shame or anger, perhaps because the others failed as well. *Not that I want them to fail. But something about not failing alone makes me feel better. Kinda. Tomorrow will be a new day with new chances.*

CHAPTER 6

July 17, 1867
Day Three

Delbert woke as the horizon began to glow. He crawled out of bed and walked toward the fire. He stopped mid-stride and watched Jed and Ross talk as they stood over snaring equipment. He rubbed his eyes in disbelief. Broken ropes now repaired and coiled lay next to buckskin pouches. Delbert rubbed the back of his neck. *I'll be.* The boys were never this excited nor ready.

He glanced down toward the creek and thought about taking another stab at building more fish traps. *I need shallow water, and not just one trap, but several. Up and down the creek. Different spots. Ma's right, "Don't put all your eggs in one basket."* He chuckled at Pekam's famous, yet annoying proverb, "Don't put all your arrows in one quiver." *But it doesn't seem like nonsense now.*

Delbert looked around and felt something missing. *Bait. I need more crickets.* He knew snatching them from the dew covered grass would be tougher than expected, so he'd need to enlist the help of the other two. He grunted, knowing it might take a bit to get the boys to comply with

43

his plan. But it was worth a try. And knowing Jed and Ross were as hungry as he was, probability was in his favor. He looked over at Jed's tent and spotted extra pouches and scraps of bread.

"Gonna need your help, boys," Delbert said.

Ross grunted. "What for? We're busy, can't you see?"

"Yeah. I can. But I have to catch more crickets and it's easier with help."

Jed watched Ross look for approval.

"What do ya say, Jed?" Delbert asked.

Jed shifted his gaze to Delbert. "Okay, I reckon."

"Ross?" Delbert pleaded. "I'll waste too much time trying to catch these critters by myself."

"Fine. But we can't take too long. We need to get these snares up. I'm hungry," Ross said. "The critters around here'll be headin' for water soon. We need to get movin'."

Delbert smiled. "Thanks. This'll speed things up." He saw Ross's lips move, although he couldn't hear the words. Didn't much care. He was thankful for the extra hands.

Before they left to catch crickets, Delbert gave his friends a quick lesson on the art of capturing live crickets. "It's all in your wrist. You have to sneak up on them real slow like. Be patient. They like woodpiles and being under rocks and boulders. Listen for their chirping, too. Here, lemme show you." He ignored their snickers.

"This'll be easy," Ross snorted. He and Jed practiced flicking their wrists and made chirping noises. "Come on, Jed. Let's get goin'. We need to get this over and git back to real skills like huntin'."

Delbert watched them walk away. He brushed off Ross's flippant attitude. He was too hungry to care. "I'm sure they'll take me serious," he said loud enough for them to hear. He headed south and followed Hall Creek, not only to catch crickets, but also in search of suitable sticks to form traps and spear bait.

He daydreamed about rocks during a half-mile trek, wondering if he could find some quartz or gypsum. He knew he could find volcanic and basalt rock. Couldn't wait to do a hardness test. "I'll bring various samples home and compare them with what I already have." He studied rock after rock. His neck felt like the sun was scorching it. "How dim-witted of me to forget my Stetson. Can't believe I left it back at the Sinyekst village."

Sticks. Fish.

His attention returned to the task at hand. He collected several sticks and inspected them for size and strength. Then he headed back to the sandy beach. He inserted the sticks into the shore and worked his way out into the water, one by one, alternating sizes and diameters to form the heart shape at the top. He made five traps in different locations along the shoreline. This time he kept them out of the swift current.

"Perfect spot for fish to have a nice pool to hang around and wait for their execution. I can already feel my belly fillin' up." He hummed as he worked.

Delbert's mouth watered as he envisioned trout with bellies as red as Indian Paint Brush sliding down his throat. His famished body screamed for food. He felt like a wilting flower in summer heat.

All I need now is bait. He returned to camp and searched for Jed and Ross. He saw no movement.

45

Delbert's heart raced. His knees wobbled from hunger. The last of the food had been devoured for breakfast. He crouched down and cupped some water in his blistered hands. He sipped it. Let the coolness slide down his throat. Then scooped up some more and poured it on the back of his neck.

Still kneeling, he half prayed and half talked to himself. "We're on our own now. We have to pass this test. I refuse to go home whipped. I will succeed—no matter the cost."

Delbert decided to look for the others and help them capture more crickets. He heard a few chirps in the distance where downfall was arranged like the aftermath of a windstorm. He walked close, stopped, and crouched down as if a hungry mountain lion. He crept toward a large piece of ponderosa pine and pressed his nose inches from the fissured bark that looked like deep gulches. He waited. The bark had a tinge of orange to it. Soon a pair of tiny antennas peeked over the top of the log. *Lookee there.*

Delbert held his breath. His lungs began to burn. He blew the air down his chin. The cricket froze like a stone statue for a few moments, then eased over the log within reach. Delbert lifted his hand so slow it went undetected. For a couple seconds anyhow. The cricket turned away. He froze, feeling his chest move air in and out. A deer leaped out of the brush. *Wait!* The cricket hopped away.

Back to worms.

A tug of worry swirled in his gut, twisting his thoughts.

"Suppose I'll try crickets later. Morning's the best time, if they come out at all. Hope it's not pouring rain or nothin'll be out. What's the use? Maybe we should just eat the worms." He sighed.

Upon his return to camp, he located his shovel and headed for dirt. Fat worms soon appeared on the tip of the shovel. He put one up to his lips and hesitated. *No. I better use 'em for bait.* He slid worms into the slit of the five sticks and jabbed them into the center of the fish trap. The worms slid in easy. They wiggled in the water and it made him laugh. After he tested the sturdiness of the traps, he decided to go mineral hunting. "The other two are still out, so what do I have to lose? I bet they gave up and went snaring. I sure hope they catch a rabbit or martin. Anything, really."

Ross felt rage bubble inside. "Can you believe Delbert? Flick of the wrist. I betcha he doesn't catch even one *stupid* cricket."

"I'll bet he catches a lot. I've seen 'im do it plenty."

"When?"

"Last summer at his place. We were out gathering wood for his Ma. Sun was settin' and they were loud. Surrounded us." Jed shook his head. "He's quick with that wrist flicking, I'll tell you."

Ross crunched his face like a dried apple. "Yeah, real quick. I bet. Delbert's too stocky to be quick. It's skinny guys like me that are fast. And you?" He looked Jed up and down. "You're good for plucking jars off tall shelves for our mamas."

Jed punched Ross in the gut. "I'm good at a lot more than that!"

"Like what?"

"I'm…"

"That's what I thought."

Jed punched Ross in the same place. Ross hunched over and groaned.

"Don't need to explain myself to you," Jed said. "Should've went with Delbert. He's a lot funner than you."

"All Del does is second guess himself. How is that fun?"

"He doesn't second guess himself. He knows a lot of stuff. More than me or you. He reads all them books. He's just more like his Ma than his Pa."

Ross straightened himself. "That he is. But his Pa don't care. Phillip thinks each man should follow what God intends for him. Not me though. I'm following in my Pa's footsteps. I'm gonna be a rancher, too."

"Yeah, you better stick to cows and marry a woman who's a good cook, 'cause you can't seem to fend for yourself."

Ross took off after Jed. But with Jed's long legs, he didn't have a prayer to catch him.

As the sun set high in the sky, Delbert sat against a larch tree and inspected his new rock collection. He heard the crackle of twigs in the distance and jumped to his feet. His pulse raced.

"Get anything?" He added a few sticks and fanned the pitiful flames of a smoldering fire.

Ross lifted a brown fur ball into the air. "We got one!"

Jed slapped Ross on the back. "Yeah, nice rabbit, Ross."

"Nice work, boys." Delbert handed his knife to Ross.

"Just like Pekam said," Jed exclaimed. "This boy's tracks led right to his watering hole. It worked like a snap. Sorry about the crickets. We never did hear any, so we just went to settin' snares."

Delbert nodded. "I figured so. I tried to catch one, but it got away when a deer bound outta the brush. So I gave up and thought worms would be quicker."

"And?" Jed asked.

"They were!" Delbert laughed.

Ross laughed, too, but not at Delbert this time. He skinned the rabbit in record time.

Delbert found three long sticks and handed them over to Jed and Ross who speared slabs of fresh meat on the ends and roasted them over the fire. The aroma of sizzling meat wafted in the air and wedged in Delbert's nose. He joked and laughed with his friends as they waited. Hungry. Anxious.

The meat lasted about as long as it took to spear it.

Delbert sat and stared at the other two. He was thankful for the food, but still hungry. By the look on their faces, Ross and Jed were also. The three stood in unison, without saying a word, and raced to the creek. Delbert rushed to one fish trap for inspection, not stopping to remove his cowboy boots and saw the other two do the same. He peered into the trap and found nothing. Heat rose up his neck as he slapped his leg.

49

Jed waved them over to another trap. He jumped and hollered in a high-pitched shrill, trying to remain upright as his boots slid over slimy rocks. A speckled trout with a red streak running down its sides rested in the tip of the trap.

Delbert rushed over and leaned close, letting loose a howl. He lost his balance and slammed into the creek. His shoulder cracked against the rocky bottom. He felt no pain. *I did it. I caught a fish.* He scrambled upright and balanced against the current.

Ross rushed over to see Delbert's catch.

Jed ran to the other three traps. "Empty here," he called out.

"At least you caught one," Ross said.

Delbert clambered to his feet and gave Ross a grateful smile. He felt relief flood his face. This was no time to rib a friend. But it was time to thank their Creator.

Delbert picked up his catch with both hands and held the trout knowing his life depended on it. His heart thrummed with pride. "Come on, let's stoke the fire and roast this thing."

They sat by the fire, hands up and with their drenched boots propped up against the rocks. They listened to the fire crackle. Watched the flames lick their fish.

The sun slid halfway behind the western mountains and as it did so the cricket chorus came alive as if to tease Delbert. While boots steamed by the fire, Delbert convinced Ross and Jed to join him and attempt to catch those annoying critters. He sat taller and stretched his neck as he scouted the terrain. He instructed Jed and Ross to sneak around barefoot, which he decided was quieter, and pointed them in different directions.

Before they left, Delbert reviewed the cricket snatching instructions.

Jed snickered.

Ross rolled his eyes.

Ross and Jed listened with smirks on their faces. Once again, Delbert ignored their brashness.

Ross flicked his wrist. "Like this?"

Jed laughed. "What about this call?" He cupped is hands over his mouth and made a high-pitched chirping noise.

Delbert sat for a moment and watched their reaction. He challenged them by asking, "Okay, I bet you two don't catch one cricket. But here's the deal, whoever's cricket snags a red skinned trout, gets to eat it. The others starve."

"You're on," Jed and Ross exclaimed in unison.

Delbert turned on his heels and headed north.

Ross turned west and Jed headed south, just as they were instructed.

Later Delbert rendezvoused with the other two at the edge of the creek. The glowing moon lit the sky and led the way. Delbert had three crickets. Ross had one. Jed had none. Delbert held his tongue even though he felt like he could explode from such a strong and satisfying pleasure. *I got 'em now!*

They reset the bait and decided to check for results in the morning.

Delbert tossed and turned. The desire to beat them at their own game consumed his thoughts. But after what seemed an hour, his body relaxed and his breathing

51

slowed.

The crickets continued to sing.

July 18, 1867
Day Four

Delbert tossed back and forth as daylight pierced his eyes. Unable to sleep, he dressed and crawled out of his tent. He heard the other two snoring. The mountain air smelled fresh. The sound of the creek called to him. He listened a moment longer before he stretched his stiff, cold muscles and rushed to the traps.

His belly bellowed and his mouth watered. First trap, none. Second trap, empty. Third, forth, and fifth traps, zero. Delbert sank to the ground. His mood was as gloomy as the storm clouds rolling in from the northern horizon. *Failure, that's what you are.* The words crept into the cracks of his unguarded mind. They hadn't whispered their haunting voices for days. Now these empty traps surrounded him as though a testament of his weakness. *Yes, nothing but a failure. I let myself down. I let Pekam down. I let my pa down. I let the boys down.*

He sat in the wet sand with his head between his knees. His body shook with anger. "I can't give up this soon. There has to be a way. I know this can work. It has to. Pekam and his people fish this way all the time. The small children in his village even do it." He spoke as if the good Lord sat beside him. He searched the heavens and sighed. "You'll carry me through. You promise in Your word. You're not a liar. I haveta trust you and throw my emotions to the wind." He scanned the rock faces that poked through the thick curtain of conifer trees.

"Okay, God. You say when we commit our needs and dreams to You, they *will* come to pass. So here I sit. I need to catch fish. I…we need to survive…by ourselves…please let this come to pass. I know we can live off the land with all you have created for us…"

He watched the leaves of the quaking aspen ripple in the breeze as if to encourage him. "Get up. Keep going" is what they seemed to say. His mind flashed images of him watching Pekam. He and some other men walked up a stream and pushed fish toward traps. The same traps he'd made.

Delbert jumped to his feet and sprinted to camp. He shook each tent, even his own in the wake of excitement and yelled, "Get up!"

Jed popped his head out first, a grumpy frown on his face.

Ross attempted to open his blinking eyes.

"Come on. Get dressed. Daylights a burnin'. We've got work to do."

Ross rolled over on his back and groaned. "What're you babbling about?"

"The traps are empty, but I have a plan." Delbert shook the tents until the boys crawled out. "Pekam spoke to me. No, God did, through Pekam."

Jed's sleepy eyes strained to focus. "What?"

"This better be worth it," Ross sneered.

"I was sure there would be fish in at least one of them. But listen, when I was young, I saw Pekam and his pals walk up a creek toward different types of fish traps filling 'em pretty fast. I think we should try it. It's like herding cattle, but with fish. In water."

"Now?" Jed complained. "Can't we at least give the horses a drink first?"

Delbert turned his attention to Jed. "When did you start caring about the horses' well-being?" Delbert felt hair on the back of his neck spike outward, so he spoke in a calm, slow tone, "Did you hear me?"

"Yes, I heard you. Did you hear *me*? It's early. I wanna finish sleepin'."

"Sure ya do." Ross walked off.

"Hey, we can water the horses. Then how 'bout trying to catch some breakfast. How'd ya like worms for breakfast? If you're really fast, maybe you can snatch a grasshopper or two with a flick of your tongue. I'll start callin' ya frog, or does toad suit ya? Or would ya like to go on a Sunday afternoon stroll?" Delbert felt his patience leave his body as quickly as his last meal disappeared from his fish-oiled fingers.

Ross glared at him.

Delbert held out his hands. "You got a better idea? We're outta of food. You think it's gonna magically drop on our plates, cooked and all?" His tone sounded as impatient as a hungry wolf.

"Well, no…" Ross slouched and rubbed his eyes.

"Well, let's get goin'." Delbert marched toward the beach. He sat on the cool, damp sand, tore off his boots, and rolled up his pants. He slid the tip of his toe in and shivered.

Jed grunted and followed. He sat beside Delbert and peeled off his socks.

Ross straggled behind. He sat a spell before he

yanked off his boots and rolled up his pants, grumbling about the injustice. "Maybe we need to cut off the legs of our britches. I have a feeling we may be in there—a lot." He tilted his head toward the creek.

Delbert stared at his bare feet. *No need to stir those two up any more than they already are.* "Okay. Let's walk downstream a ways, check things out, and meander back up."

"Yep." Ross's eyebrow twitched. "Whatever you say, boss."

Ross'll be eatn' his words soon enough.

Jed followed, still rubbing the sleep out of his eyes. He slid his tongue over his cracked, swollen lips.

They tiptoed along the creek several yards and dodged pinecones and sticks, grimacing at sharp rocks that carved into the bottom of their feet. Delbert mentally stopped himself from picking up prospective gems for his collection that caught his eye through the sparkle of water. *I'll for sure come back later.*

"What about here?" Ross suggested.

Delbert peered upstream. He wanted to walk a bit further, but decided to keep the peace. "Good enough." His pa taught him to pick his battles. Even though he knew Pa was referring to a disagreement with Ma, Delbert figured the same could apply to a friend as well.

Delbert slid off a short bank and Ross and Jed followed suit. The water rose above their ankles at the point of entry, but the rocks were slick and hard to maneuver. They trudged up the creek, arms out to keep their balance. Ross and Jed rustled fir branches in the water. Delbert plunged his hand in and scooped up a handful of pebbles. He tossed them ahead one at a time

55

in all directions.

Finally Delbert reached the closest trap. He gestured for the other two to fan out and check additional traps. They nodded.

"None here," Ross hollered.

"One over here." Jed raised a victorious arm in the air.

"I got one!" Delbert clapped his hands and added, "Reckon we'll be eating breakfast, Jed."

Jed laughed and looked at Ross who shrugged.

"Ha, ha, you two are full of laughs," he exclaimed, his voice sounded pleading.

Delbert raced back to camp and sparked a fire. Ross and Jed trailed behind. Delbert had been smart enough to keep some of the wood and tinder dry in their tents. Soon a fire blazed and fish sizzled.

"Great. Congratulations to ya both. You can be called experts now." Ross smirked at them.

Delbert grinned at Jed, and handed a piece of fish to Ross. "You didn't really believe we'd leave ya out, did ya?"

"Nah. Much obliged."

The trio devoured fresh trout.

They laughed and joked as they nibbled on bones and picked off every last bit of meat while licking their fingers.

But soon their bellies grumbled for more. A feeling of disappointment crept through the cracks of Delbert's victory. Unspoken glances took on a serious tone. He glanced at empty palms. "It's time to take this expedition more seriously–or we're gonna starve."

CHAPTER 7

"Jed and I'll hike back into the woods and set some more snares," Ross said.

Delbert wanted to build more fish traps upstream where the current dawdled and shallow pools were more abundant. "I wanna test cricket against grasshopper against worm. I bet worms will be the best bait." He rubbed his hands as he sat by the fire, going over the plan in his mind.

"Up for a wager?" Ross asked.

"Sure. Whacha thinkin?" Delbert's expression brightened.

"Whoever wins gets outta the day's chores. Gets ta do whatever he pleases."

"Being you seem to always want out of the day's chores, I should bet somethin' different."

Jed said, "That works for me."

"I do my share of chores," Ross said through clenched teeth.

"They why are you so defensive?" Delbert asked.

Ross leaned forward. "You got a better wager?"

"This bet sounds just fine," Jed said. "You guys keep

wasting time."

"Fine. I'm stickin' with worms. What are you two gonna bet on?" Delbert asked the boys.

Jed grinned, showing deep dimples. "I'll take crickets."

"I got grasshoppers," Ross whined. "So, are we meetin' back up to go herb and root hunting in what… near high sun?" He shaded his eyes against the rising sun.

Delbert shook his head. "You couldn't judge daylight if a sunbeam slapped you in the nose—"

"Watch yourself, Del," Ross said.

Delbert pumped his fist.

"Let's go!" Jed shoved Delbert. "Come on."

Delbert grunted and took a few steps forward. His ma was an expert with herbs and roots, as were Spupaleena and Pekam. He'd paid attention here and there. "I guess it's time to see how much I learned," he said to Jed. "Ross won't get nothing but fancy talk."

Jed laughed. "I'll water the horses real quick."

Thinking on yesterday's catch put a bounce in Delbert's steps. A renewed confidence coursed through his body. His laughter was strong and he felt a sense of humor bubbling forth.

"High sun's all right with me," Delbert agreed.

He watched the horses as they snorted and swatted flies with their tails. He watched Jed untie and lead them over for a drink before tethering them for the morning. Once their four-legged friends had their fill, Jed secured them and strolled back to the creek. The horses watched the boys as if taking wagers on who would come back with what.

"At least they have plenty of green grass to eat. Glad I don't have to worry 'bout them."

"Glad I don't have to worry about you feeding us," Ross said. He spat on the ground.

Delbert looked upstream as he ignored Ross's comment. "Before we take off, let's try one more hand at pushing fish into the existing traps. There're more pools. Maybe those fish'll double back and swim against the current, smack dab into our traps." Delbert's mind imprinted an image of frying fish. His mouth watered.

"I suppose it's worth a try," Ross agreed.

Delbert looked back and saw the horses had stopped chewing. They watched as Ross and Jed hopped into the creek. He turned to follow and heard them snort and rip grass with sharp teeth.

Jed headed downstream with sticks and pebbles in-hand.

Delbert led the way as he and Ross aimed upstream. They clutched fir branches in both fists.

Ross swatted at gnats and closed his mouth. He felt one rolling around on his tongue and swallowed it. "You can also use the needles as barriers if the fish try to dart past you," he mentioned. "As long as I can catch these dang-nabbed fish."

Delbert jerked as his tender feet touched smooth, slippery rocks. The current pushed and pulled at him. But he trudged on. The icy, burning sensation on his feet and ankles faded into numbness.

He watched Jed and Ross perform their trout-gathering dance. He hoped it would bring an abundant catch as they splashed through the creek. Once at the traps, Delbert peered in. Nothing.

His shoulders slumped. His gloom turned to frustration as he heard Ross slap the water's surface with branches.

Delbert shoved his hands to his hips and spoke to himself, "What'd we do wrong?"

Ross pushed against the current to check another trap. "Nothing here," he hollered.

Jed hopped from one trap to the other. He leaned down and peered into a trap. "Hang on, you–" A log rushed past and slammed into Jed's head. It knocked him into the current.

"Jed, look out!" Delbert ran for his friend. His feet slipped on slimy rocks and he fell. A mouthful of water gushed in and he felt as if he was drowning. His chest tightened. Water swirled around him and he opened his eyes. All he saw were bubbles and rushing water. He surfaced. Water slipped down his throat and he spit and sputtered. The current captured him and carried his flailing body downstream. He twisted around and anchored his feet into some thick mud at the edge of the creek bed and managed to stand. He trudged upstream toward Jed, lungs on fire. He shivered as he walked against sopping clothes. He mopped his eyes with his soaked shirtsleeve and licked his cracked lips.

Ross got to Jed first and was able to take hold of Jed's shirt collar and reel him onto shore. "He's conscious but talkin' funny," Ross hollered over his shoulder.

A red stream ran down Jed's face and neck. A red circle stained his shirt.

Delbert helped Ross drag Jed onto dry ground. They panted. They heaved.

"My ankle. I think I twisted it," Jed slurred. He

wiggle his toes and winced at the pain. "I felt it pop."

"Your head looks bad," Delbert said.

"Huh?" Jed explored his head with trembling fingers. He pressed his hand against the wound. "Boy, my skull hurts. Guess we need to stop this bleedin'."

Delbert grasped Jed's heel in one hand and his friend's calf in the other, holding on with open fingers. "It doesn't look broke, but sure is turning purple. Fast. And it's pretty swollen."

Jed's hand slammed to the ground as he tried to shift his weight. "Ouch!"

Ross's brows furrowed. "You all right?"

Jed nodded.

Delbert scanned Jed's ankle like a doctor examines a patient. "That looks bad. Stick it back in the creek. Let the cold water do its job." He saw the pain in Jed's expression. His clenched jaw was a telltale. Delbert fingered Jed's hair to find the point of impact. "This is nothing, a flesh wound. You'll be fine, your head, that is."

Delbert and Ross attempted a chuckle.

Jed scowled back at them as a jolt of pain stabbed at his ankle.

"Let's get him to the grass. I'll go get a blanket and some dry clothes," Ross ordered.

"Wait," Delbert said. "No. The cold water will bring the swelling down. Trust me. He needs to stay here." He glanced over his shoulder. "I think I saw a willow tree over there. I'll peel some bark off it. It'll help with the pain and swelling. I'll go find it as soon as we get him settled."

"Yeah, I saw it. I'll go with you." Ross jogged to the

tents to fetch a blanket and a couple of coats, one for Jed's head and the other to prop under his ankle.

"We haveta move you a little to get these wet clothes off, then gonna have to scoot ya back to the creek." He eyed Jed and searched for objection.

"Yeah, I know. Let's just get it over with." Jed held his breath and let Delbert drag him up on the bank. Jed pushed against the muddy ground with his good foot.

They peeled off Jed's wet clothes and slid on dry ones. Delbert eased the pant leg over Jed's sprained ankle and glided a folded jacket under his knee. Ross positioned the other jacket under his head and drew a blanket over him. Jed shivered in the warm summer morning.

Delbert and Ross inched Jed closer to the creek.

Delbert turned away as he lowered Jed's swollen, purple ankle in the icy creek. He felt queasy at the sight of it. A dizzy spell washed over him as he tried to stand. He splayed his arms out until it passed.

When Jed was as comfortable as possible, Delbert grabbed Ross and hightailed it to fetch the willow bark for tea.

"Don't be too long. The pain's bad." Jed moaned. "I'm aching somethin' fierce."

"I hate leavin' 'im," Ross said.

"Yeah, me, too, but we need to get the bark and some roots. I'm starving, and I bet Jed's stomach's grumblin' more than ours now."

Ross nodded.

Delbert led the way to a couple big willow trees. He cut and peeled sections of bark and tucked them in a buckskin pouch his ma made them for the adventure.

Delbert ran his fingers over the tight, even stitches.

Ross picked some plants that grew by the willows. "Hey, here's some Cow Parsnip. It tastes like celery." He inhaled the acrid scent. "Huh? This is supposed to smell sweet." He handed some to Delbert.

Delbert sniffed the plant. "No, this can't be it. Put it down."

Ross licked the stem. Took a small bite.

Delbert slapped it out of his hand. "What're ya doin'? This could be poisonous."

"I'm sure it's not."

Delbert felt his face grow hot. "I wish you'd listen for once."

Ross shrugged as he watched water drip off his pant leg onto his boots. "Yeah, you're always right, aren't ya?" He snorted. "Ya look pretty messy for somebody sittin' so tall in the saddle."

Delbert brushed off his damp, muddy clothing. "Don't really matter none out here. Let's hurry and get back."

Delbert finished cutting out squares of willow bark from the tree trunk and scavenged for roots and berries before hurrying back.

On the way to camp, Ross tapped Delbert on the shoulder and pointed to a sunflower. "The seeds are good eatin'."

"Yeah. We should hunt for duck eggs, too. We could fry some up. We did bring a pan, right?"

"I think Jed did. I'll check his pack when we get back. If not, we have our cups to cook 'em with."

"I s'pose if we get desperate, we can pick that black

moss from tamaracks and steam it overnight and into the morning. Don't taste bad."

"If we get desperate," Ross said.

At camp, Delbert mashed up the inside of the willow bark and made a poultice.

Jed held his breath as Delbert wrapped his ankle with strips from one of Ross's shirts. "Ouch. Be careful." He pulled his foot back as an electric *zing* shot up his leg.

Delbert handed him a sliver of willow bark. "Here, chew on this."

"Really?" Jed placed it in his mouth.

"No. Not really," Delbert groaned.

Jed spit out the hunk of bark in the sand.

"Why'd you do that? I was being sarcastic." Delbert chuckled and continued to doctor Jed.

Jed picked up the piece of bark, wiped it on his pants, and slipped it back in his mouth.

Ross left to cut fir boughs for soft support.

"I'll make some tea outta the rest"— Delbert tilted his head in the direction of the slice of willow bark he cut from the tree—"it should ease the pain."

Jed yelped.

"Sorry. I'm tryin' to be as careful as I can." Delbert wrapped faster.

"Here're the boughs." Ross dropped them beside Jed. A puff of dust floated up.

Delbert flashed him a scowl. He tied the cloth off and eased Jed's ankle on top a stack of fir boughs.

"I feel like I could eat an entire hindquarter of a moose," Jed admitted.

"Good. I'll have a little somethin' for ya to eat soon." Delbert sat a moment to study Jed. "You rest. Me and Ross'll go set some snares." He sat back on his ankles and stared into the creek. "I need to figure those fish traps out. I just don't get why they keep coming up empty."

Delbert tossed Jed a buckskin pouch. "I found these wild carrots for you while Ross was taking care of business in the bushes. It's not the backend of a moose, but it'll have to do."

Jed scooped up the pack and peeked inside. He shoved them into his mouth.

"Did you even taste 'em?"

Jed grinned. He swallowed and dipped his head to help the pieces slide down his dry throat. "Gonna get some more?"

"I'll try. We were kinda in a rush to get back." Delbert nodded toward Jed's ankle.

"Hey, Delbert…" Ross stood with his face in his hands.

"What?"

"Sum thin'th rong."

"You sound like you snuck some medicine from Pekam's grumpy healer. The kind she uses to knock people out." He turned to Jed. "She's scary."

Ross waved him over.

"More than likely a trick." Jed grunted.

"Could be." Delbert narrowed his eyes as he ambled toward camp. He moved closer and his eyes widened. His jaw dropped. "What happened to you?"

Ross's mouth and tongue were puffed up. Glazed, wild-looking eyes stared back at him. His skin red as an apple.

Delbert helped Ross sit down. "Can you breathe okay?"

Ross nodded. Then shook his head.

"Can you swallow?"

Ross shrugged. "Thorta." His tongue so enlarged the words squeaked out. He nodded again.

"Okay. You're having some sorta reaction. My ma warned me about this. Hold on. I gotta make sure I get the right one." Delbert slid the knife out of his pocket and cut a Ponderosa pine branch.

"What's going on up there?" Jed asked, having to yell to be heard. Impatience engulfed him.

"Ross's been poisoned," Delbert hollered back.

"How?"

"He licked some Water Hemlock."

"Some what?"

Delbert tensed as he tried to decide if he had the right species of trees. "Hang on. I gotta figure this out."

Delbert handed the branch to Ross and told him to bite off a piece of the end. Ross opened his mouth and clenched his teeth on the bark. He bit off the end and chewed. His eyes teared and he shook his head.

"Spit it out!" Delbert said.

Ross muttered something, but Delbert couldn't decipher it.

"I think I need the Douglas fir." Delbert fetched a branch and brought it to Ross.

Ross bit off the end and began chewing. Within a couple minutes, the swelling began to subside.

Relief shown on Jed's face.

"I'll get you somethin' to drink."

Ross tried to swallow, but he gagged instead. "Much obliged," he whispered.

Delbert grabbed a tin cup and sprinted to the creek past Jed.

"You gonna let me in on this?" Jed asked.

"Shortly."

Jed threw a pinecone at him. "When?"

Delbert carried the cup to Ross with tiny steps and made sure he could swallow a sip.

Ross clutched his throat. "I'm going to go lie down." He handed the cup back to Delbert and attempted to stand. Delbert clung to his arm and held him steady until he regained his balance. The cup toppled to the ground. Ross got his bearings, wobbled to his tent, and dropped to his blanket. He hit it with a loud *thud*, rolled over, and groaned.

Delbert set the cup on a log and checked on Jed. "I'm going to set some snares. You want me to drag you up by the fire?"

"No. I'm fine here. So, what happened to the herb gatherer?"

Delbert filled Jed in on Ross's mishap. He paused to hand Jed a cup of water.

Jed laughed. "I thought I was bad." He flinched when he moved his ankle. "I'll just keep the ground warm and watch over these here traps. Maybe I'll sing one of Pekam's huntin' songs. Never know. It could get them trout to swim upstream." Jed thought a moment. "Is there a fishin' song Pekam sings? I reckon I could give

67

that a try."

Delbert slapped Jed's shoulder. "You can always make one up. I'm taking my horse. It'll do him some good to get some exercise."

Jed stretched out and closed his eyes. "See ya when you get back." He hummed a sore account of a Sinyekst chant.

Delbert tacked up and faced his bay gelding, "Let's go, boy." He tied the other two horses on a picket line so they wouldn't try and follow. He hoisted himself into the saddle and reined his gelding around. Headed north, he didn't look back.

CHAPTER 8

Delbert ground tied Charlie in a grassy clearing surrounded by a patch of orange wild lilies. He grabbed a couple ropes out of his leather saddlebag that looked like rats had tried to have them for a meal. He tucked one under his arm, tugged on the other, and felt it give. "No wonder they didn't snag anything." He snapped the ends. It broke. He flung the halves aside and grabbed the other and did the same. It also broke. Once he'd chucked those halves to the dirt, he scanned the ground, brush, and trees, searching for something he could use. But there were only green leaves and black moss. *Plants with vines haven't come up yet. No cattails either.*

He plopped down on a log and cradled his head in his hands. "God, what else could go wrong? I swear, I'm nothin' but a greenhorn." He rubbed his head and groaned.

This little pity party took him nowhere so he scanned the trees and bushes for vine, bark, anything he could use to make a rope. *I've gotta be missing somethin'.* He sucked in a deep breath and felt his body relax as clean air burst into his lungs. He hoped his mind would clear and allow ideas and solutions to float in. The ropes scratched his hands as he tucked them into his saddlebag.

Charlie whickered. Delbert sauntered over and stroked his soft, brown hair. He rustled the horse's black mane, his gaze shifting to the black tail that stretched to the ground. Delbert walked to the gelding's hindquarters. "Long black tail, of course."

He pulled out his knife and cut off a hunk of hair from the middle of Charlie's tail that was as thick as his pinky and tied the ends together. The hair felt coarse, strong. It would do. He stared at the length of horsehair for some time and pondered how to braid it. He'd watched his ma work with his sister's long, thick hair, but never did get around to braiding much himself. Never saw a need. He spotted an apple-sized rock, picked it up, and tossed it in the air. "Yep, it's heavy enough." He sat on a downed tree with his feet on the rock and anchored the horsetail underneath it. His fingers fumbled as he tried to braid the three strands into a rope. He cursed. His stubby fingers just made a mess of it so he unbraided the rope and started over.

Delbert caught himself humming, just like his mother did when she worked. He loved to hear her sweet, angelic voice. He missed their late night talks. Steaming apple pie. His gut clenched. He ignored the pain and continued to braid.

When he got the hang of things, braiding the hair was a snap. He tied the ends, jumped to his feet, and plodded to the edge of the creek in search of rabbit or squirrel trails. He walked upstream through brushy terrain and found little feet that carved a trail to the left. *A rabbit? A squirrel? A mouse?*

At this point he didn't care much what he captured. *Anything I can cook and eat'll do.* His stomach felt hollow.

Lips dry and chapped. Licking them made it worse.

Water. What fool would forget water? Delbert held up a hand. "I'm the fool." He ripped out a handful of juicy, green grass and chewed on it. The moisture from the blades refreshed his parched mouth.

Once the horsehair was braided, tight enough to get the job done, he found a sapling near the edge of a narrow small game trail and lopped a few feet off the top. With his braided cord he formed a loop and held it up to the palm of his hand. Just right. He tied the rope to one end of the sapling and shoved the other end into the ground at an angle. He studied the foliage on the sapling and decided it needed to come off so he stripped it bare. He found two thin, long twigs and snapped them from their branches. He inserted them inside each end of the loop and sank them into the ground, holding the loop in place.

He stood and admired his work. He looked at his hands, sniffed them, and knew if animals smelled human flesh they'd run. So he found some mud by the creek, scooped up a handful and washed the sticks with it, praying his scent would at least be masked. He wiped his hands on his pants and knew he had to start over. This time, he wiped his hands on grass. He made his way back to Charlie, who stomped his feet, swished his tail, and flung his head back and forth like an angry bull, trying to keep flies at bay.

Delbert mopped the sweat from his brow with the back of his hand and licked his dry, cracked lips. He grimaced as the salt in his saliva stung and reached for more lush grass and popped a handful in his mouth. "Wish I had some of Ma's salve and somethin' to drink," he spoke to Charlie, "and by the looks of it, so do you."

The bay pawed the ground with swift strikes. Delbert ran one hand down the gelding's neck, talking to him in soothing tones, and swatted at flies with the other hand. He snuck one last look at the snare and knew he had no choice but to either locate a spring or waterfall, or turn back. He brushed hair out of his face. "I should've made the snares closer to camp. What was I thinking?" He slapped Charlie's shoulder and watched a dead fly drop to the ground.

Charlie sucked in his gut as Delbert snatched up the reins and tightened the cinch. He climbed into the saddle and urged his gelding east. "East? Is that right? I reckon it'll be a stab in the dark. What do you think, ol' boy?" Charlie snorted and shook flies from his ears. Delbert searched the area, wising he'd paid better attention to his surroundings.

They traveled for what seemed like miles with no luck. His dry mouth begged for something wet. *Anything.* His stomach screamed. He grew weak, too dizzy to hold on to the saddle horn and focus on the trail. *East.* "Don't think I can find the snare again, ol' boy. Are we gonna starve?" He patted the horse's neck. "Can we survive off eating grass? I s'pose if it's good enough for you, it's good enough for me."

Delbert and Charlie wandered around for a while before Delbert got the urge to turn a different direction.

"I think we need to turn around, Charlie. Not so sure this is the way back to camp." Delbert reined him back around. Charlie's ears pricked forward and he broke into a trot. Delbert leaned to the right. "Whoa, boy, my head's spinin'." He bounced around until he found the center of the saddle and pulled back on the reins. The bay slowed to a fast walk.

"I'm tired, Charlie." He yawned. The rocking motion made his eyes heavy, but his dizziness began to subside. Delbert shook his head to stay awake, yet his eyelids closed.

Delbert blinked the sleep away. He looked around and his scrutiny rested on Charlie. "How long did you let me sleep, boy?" He realized he was sitting on the back of his horse and they were in the middle of the creek. "Where are we, anyhow?" He glanced down. "Hmm. Thanks for not dumpin' me in." He slid off the horse and sank into the shallow water and drank. Once he had his fill, he splashed its coolness on his face. He dunked his head in and came up drenched and refreshed. He felt alive and awake.

He again eyed the terrain. *I have no idea where we are.* He reached out and rubbed his horse's neck. "I hope you know the way back to camp, ol' boy."

Charlie cocked a hind leg and stood relaxed. He blew air from his nose and lowered his head with his lids half closed. Delbert watched him. "You're in no hurry, are ya?"

He uncinched the saddle right there in the water, set it on a log, and rubbed his four-legged friend down with handfuls of grass. Charlie pawed the ground and splashed cool water on Delbert. He didn't mind, but hoped his horse wouldn't roll. He let Charlie rest in the creek until sweat dried from his back. Charlie resisted at first when Delbert tried to lead him out, but a patch of lush grass seemed to convince the horse it was okay. Charlie bent his head down, pulled up thick blades, and chewed. He blinked and rubbed flies off his nose with his leg, went back to chewing.

Delbert leaned against a tree and closed his eyes.

Lord, which way do I head back to camp?

The sun hung high and blistered the earth below when Delbert awoke. "It's gotta be mid-afternoon. How do ya think the boys are holding up, ol' boy, huh? Think they've eaten? Think there're fish in the traps?" He glanced at Charlie and waited for any hint of comprehension. Delbert stroked his neck. "Yep, gonna have to trust you to get us back to camp."

It didn't take long to saddle the bay and get back on the trail. Delbert let Charlie pick his way through the trees. He felt tension in his back and butt as he prayed Charlie knew the way.

Soon he began to recognize the terrain as he rocked in the saddle to Charlie's laid-back stride. He remembered the dead tree to the right and the grove of quaking aspen up ahead. His heart fluttered. He reached down to stroke the horse's neck, emotion tightening his throat, "We made it!" Horses whinnied and Charlie's ears flickered back and forth as he picked up the pace. Delbert slapped his leg. "Ya done good, ol'boy."

Delbert hollered at the boys and Ross stood to greet him.

"What took ya so long?" Ross searched his friend for signs of fresh meat.

Delbert looked away. He fiddled with the reins. "Uh, I had some trouble."

"What kind of trouble?"

"Where's Jed?" Delbert asked.

"Over here." Jed's voiced sounded garbled.

Delbert twisted around in the saddle. He found Jed lounged in the shade of an old ponderosa pine on a thick bed of fir boughs with a sleepy smirk. "What's with him?"

"I reckon the willow bark's doing its job and warding off the pain. I boiled a bunch and gave it to 'im."

Delbert's eyes widened. "How much?"

"Not that much." Ross grinned. "Just enough."

Delbert looked at Ross, searching for mischief. "Must be workin'."

"Get anything?"

Delbert's gaze dropped to the ground. "Nope."

Ross stretched. "Nothin' in the fish traps, either. Where're all the fish, anyway? I figured we'd be eatin' like kings by now."

"Are ya sure?" Delbert marched to the creek with Ross on his heels. *Looks like my quiver came up empty after all.*

Delbert's jaw clenched as he gathered a handful of rocks from the creek bed and started chucking them. Rage boiled his blood. He ripped sticks out of the sand and flung them onto the bank. He screamed. He screamed at his pa. He screamed at his friends. He screamed at himself. "I'm nothing but a failure!"

Ross grabbed Delbert by the waist and tackled him. They landed in the water, hitting bottom. Delbert pushed away from Ross, stood, fist in the air, ready to punch the first thing he saw.

Ross pushed to his feet.

Delbert swung.

Ross dodged his fist and tackled him again. This time they landed on the bank. Ross pinned Delbert until he quit flailing. Ross rolled onto his back—both boys' chests heaved. They sucked in the humid air, lungs burning.

"What was that about?" Ross asked in between gasps

of air.

"Nothin'."

"Nothin'?"

Delbert grunted.

"If that was nothin', I'd hate to see somethin'."

Delbert flung a handful of rocks at Ross.

Ross dodged them. "Do ya need to cool off again?" He gave him an I-have-no-problem-throwing-you-in-the-drink-again look.

Delbert glared. "No." He scooted to the edge of the creek and splashed water on his face. "Sorry. I was a little outta sorts." He lay down and watched birds float on the airstream.

"A little?" Ross snorted.

"I'm hungry, tired, and feel like givin' up."

"So do I. But I'm not quitin'. We can't. We hav'ta get Jed back."

Delbert scanned Ross's face. "How's your lips? I see you're still a bit swollen."

Ross patted them with his fingertips. "Just a bit. Not bad, though. At least I can swallow."

"Hey, what's going on down there?" Jed's faint voice caught their attention.

They exchanged apologetic glances.

"What's goin' on?" Jed's voice grew impatient.

"Nothin'." They shouted in unison.

"I'm hungry," Jed hollered.

"So are we." Ross tossed a rock in the creek. "Time to set some snares. Again."

Delbert stood. "I'll find some more crickets…and

berries. No, none are ripe yet. Well, maybe some service berries are. Maybe Oregon grape. I'll check." Delbert snatched a basket from his tent and lit out in search of food. *It's up to me now.*

He whistled and pictured Jed and his goofy smirk and Ross's swollen face. He chuckled and he whistled some more. It felt nice.

CHAPTER 9

July 19, 1867
Day Five

Clouds boiled overhead and the scent of sumac lingered in the air. Delbert managed to catch a handful of crickets, a couple grasshoppers, and a handful of long, plump worms near camp. He considered shoving them in his mouth but decided against it. *Fish gotta taste better.*

He jostled the crickets and grasshoppers in a buckskin pouch, tied it to his belt, and tossed the worms in the basket leaning against a rock. Grass, twigs, and mud covered every inch of ground.

Midmorning crept over the mountain and his nerves felt raw. He'd better check his temper before it ignited as fast as lightening to dry grass. He was tired of wandering around in the muck. He didn't whistle or hum now. Only the sound of some black and orange birds were heard chirping in the canopy. He threw rocks at them. They ricocheted off the trees and dropped back to earth. Delbert despised the joyous sound. He slumped against a log and hugged his legs. He felt like nodding off for a moment, but the loud growl of his gut reminded him: *no time to sleep.* And those darned birds. "Shut up!" He closed his eyes tight. They were heavy. His body tense.

He forced his lids open and examined the rock profile above him that resembled an old man. Resembled Pekam's father. *How come I've never seen a woman's face or a young face?* He rubbed his brow and yawned.

Vicious words tiptoed into his mind while he stared at the male face in the distance. His smile faded to a frown as the remarks slashed his confidence. *You'll never be as good as him. How could you think surviving in the woods would be possible? You should have paid more attention to your pa. Stupid boy. Stupid boy. You should have kept your nose out of those books. How could your ma encourage you to be educated? A scholar? Stupid boy.*

Delbert wrenched his gaze from the rock outcropping. His body froze as the cruelty thrashed his mind and heart. *You're a failure. Look how your fish traps came up empty and washed downstream. Can't even set a decent snare. Stupid boy.*

Shame. Pity. Humiliation. It all washed over Delbert like a cold shower. He leaped to his feet, ready to fight those feelings off. "I am *not* a stupid boy!"

Tears welled in his eyes. He blinked them away. Bile rose in his throat as he tried to swallow and he drew in a breath filled with a mixture of anxiety and courage. He shook his head and prayed, "Lord, help me. Help us. I know you made me strong. Smart…" He scooped up a handful of sticks, snapped them in two, and threw them in the brush. He really threw them at the tormenting voices in his head. "I can do this. God can show me…" He fisted the air in refusal to surrender.

He leaned down to grab the basket and knocked it

over instead. *Stupid boy!* He shook his head, tossed the spilled worms back into the basket, and marching off with determination. "I will prove myself to the voices, to Pa, to God," he shouted. Images flashed in his mind as though they were right in front of him. He stopped and watched Pekam and his relations build a pole fence that stretched across the length of a waist-deep river. He could see himself and the boys creeping downstream toward a weir as if they chased the fish into this border. He could see the images as though they were right in front of him. He's never seen Pekam and his family chase them down, but why couldn't they? It had to work.

"That's it! This is what we need to do. Now, what did he call it?" Delbert paced for a moment.

His brows furrowed. He tilted his head to one side and rubbed the back of his neck. "A Www...I know it. A ware. A wire." Delbert pounded a fist into his open palm. "A weir. That's it. Pekam built a fishing weir. I know what it is." He hightailed it back to camp.

Delbert skidded into camp and landed in front of the fire. He watched Jed recline by the fire. Jed focused on wisps of smoke spiraling up. His purple ankle was propped up on a log and he held a cup of willow bark tea in a loose grip. His attention turned to Ross puking in the bushes. Delbert shook his head while he fought off the saliva gathering in his mouth.

They'll be as much help as a skunk in a snare. What a bunch of culls. He stood straight and stared into the orange, blue coals. "I can do this myself." A feeling of peace swept through Delbert, catching him off guard. He prayed the torment would continue to shrink into the depths of his mind like a bear hibernating for a season. "The bear has to die!" He'd need to starve it.

81

"What are you talking about?" Jed asked. "You aren't making a lick of sense."

"Oh, nothing," Delbert replied. "Just talking to myself." His heart raced as he rolled up his sleeves. *I'll show 'em.* He rushed off and ran until he came to a thick brush and it clawed at his face and arms as he tumbled down a small embankment full of purple berries. A branch slapped him in the face. "Ouch!" He landed against a log with a *thud*. He lay there with his eyes closed until the pain in this head eased. When his head quit spinning, he glanced up and grinned. "Berries." He covered his eyes with his arm. Shut out the daylight that pounded his head. He smiled at the sight of food and groaned from the pain in his head.

He licked his lips.

The growl of this stomach outweighed his throbbing head.

He crouched. Regained his balance. Stood halfway. Held his head. Stood tall. Waved like grass in a breeze and limped to a nearby bush. He picked as fast as he could and shoved a handful of the purple spheres into his parched mouth. Saliva the color of his bruised body ran down his chin like a rushing stream. The tartness caused him to pucker, but his fingers lunged for more. Three more handfuls shoved into his mouth. He ate like it was his last meal. He laughed and savored the sweet juice of the serviceberries.

Delbert fumbled for his birch bark basket, shoved the worms in his pocket, and picked berries. Within thirty minutes, the basket was filled with purple orbs, bits of branches, and a few straggling leaves. He snagged one last handful and plopped the berries in his mouth. He laughed like a half-crazed man. The kind his father said lived in

Lincoln. The kind that drank too much whiskey. His hands and mouth stained blue, there would be no tricking the others. He wiped his fingers on his shirttail.

Camp was silent. Delbert found Jed sleeping and looked around for Ross. He set the basket down by the fire and strained for the slightest sound. "Ross! Ross, where are you?" He heard the crackle of leaves and sticks in the distance. His gaze darted in all directions. "Ross?" Through the brush he spied a doe and her fawn, but they darted off.

He heard heaving in the distance and followed the wretched sound. Ross bent over a log, he emptied his stomach. Delbert covered his mouth and concentrated on a squirrel clawing its way up a tree.

"What happened?"

No answer.

"You all right?"

Ross moaned.

Delbert approached his friend, slow and easy. "Are you okay? What's wrong?"

Ross wiped his mouth with the back of his hand. "I ate some berries. Not so good either." He turned and threw up again. He pointed toward camp. "Git!"

Delbert watched him hug his gut. He turned his head and covered his mouth. When he was able to speak, he said, "You know better'n that. You've been taught what berries to eat and which to leave alone." His body jerked as it fought down the urge to puke. "Did Swan Woman

83

stick some funny herb in your pouch to make you delirious?"

"I said get outta here!"

"I need your help. I know what Pekam did to get fish."

"Later!"

Delbert grunted and walked back to camp. He sneered at Jed who snored loud enough to scare game away within a ten mile radius. "I need to pull your cozy self out of that warm tent you got. Don't you look cute tucked in by wool blankets?" He kicked the dirt.

After Delbert stacked some wood and checked on the horses, he grabbed a stick and sat by the fire. After a moment of reflection, he began to sketch the weir in the dirt. He drew. He thought. He imagined.

Squeaks of two chipmunks fighting over territory caught his attention. Around the tree they scampered, then stopped to stare each other down. Squeaked again and tore off, back to circles.

His mind snapped to Ross. "You need help?"

"No! I'm fine."

Jed stirred and mumbled from his tent.

Delbert checked on the fizzled fire. He scanned the ground for kindling. Didn't see any, so he talked to the fire like it would answer back, "I reckon it's time to fetch some wood."

He pulled out the hatchet from a nearby tree and located downfall a short distance away. He chopped and stacked. He worked until hunger depleted his energy, so he gathered up his firewood and lugged it all back to camp, scuffing the toe of his boot in the dirt. Each step felt as if rocks were tied to his ankles.

Wind blew in the scent of wild roses. His body itched from sweat and he smelled his shirt. He coughed and spit as he tried to get the stink out of his mouth. "Skunks smell sweeter than this. I need a bath." He glanced in Jed's direction before staring at Ross. "So do they. We're all smellin' a tad ripe. Besides it'll give me time to think through the weir."

He looked around for the nearest sumac bush to rub all over him, but saw none. He glanced at Charlie. "Nah, I'll settle for a good scrubbin'. It'll last longer. Wish Ma woulda stuck some lye soap in my pack. 'Course she more 'n likely wanted to teach us a lesson." Charlie snorted.

Delbert smiled, "You agreeing I stink, ol' boy?" He walked over and untied the gelding. "When the fire gets goin', I might have to wash up and take my undergarments with me. The others'll have to do their own. Even Jed. I'm more than happy to bring him some grub and willow bark juice, but washing another person's undergarments is going a might too far. Perhaps soakin' the stink out will work best. Or maybe I'll hide their clothes. And blankets. Those culls need a lesson in pullin' their own weight." He stroked Charlie's nose. "Well, maybe not Jed. He can't even walk."

Delbert walked Charlie to the creek, stripped, and led the gelding into the water. Delbert squatted and rubbed his arms and chest with grass. He shivered from the cool water. Charlie nuzzled the current before taking a long drink. "What would I need to build this thing?" His gaze searched the woods. "Poles. They'd have to be as straight as I can get them. Something to tie them all together." The creek didn't look that long. He measured it in his mind and counted how many poles he'd need. Pine and larch surrounded him. That and aspen. "Those'd be too thick. Aspen too heavy. I need thinner trunks, like...cottonwood. And light. Yes, that's what Pekam used. I think," he said, flicking water on Charlie's nose. "But then again, cottonwood stinks when it gets wet and it warps as it dries. Did they use larch? Or was it too heavy?"

Delbert washed his legs. When done he leaned against Charlie to rub his feet. Charlie backed up. Delbert lost his balance and fell in. When he gained his footing, he stared at his four-legged friend and tossed water on him. Tired eyed, Charlie nickered and sauntered up on dry land. He nibbled green shoots of grass as though he didn't have a care in the world. And he didn't.

Delbert sat on a rock and shook out his drenched hair. "Thanks, ol' boy!" He wiped water off his face and went back to examining the terrain. "What am I gonna use to tie these poles together. I know there are some nice cottonwood trees up stream, but I have no idea what I'm gonna tie them together with. What do you think?" He tossed a pebble at Charlie's hind end.

"What I also need is smaller poles, or branches, to lean the pole fence against. Pekam's weir was always at an angle. Not sure why, that's just how I remember it. What do you think I should use? Maybe I should skin Ross's horse and use its hide." Delbert cackled. "Maybe I ought to skin Ross and use his hide. Worthless buzzard."

He tossed a few flat stones across the water and watched them skip.

Back at camp, Delbert gathered a handful of pine needles, dry grass, moss and green, algae-like lichen off a nearby tree. He tossed the fire fuel into the warm coals and fanned the pile with a branch from a pine tree. It didn't take long until a small flame licked at the fuel. He added small pinecones until the flames could handle kindling. Soon the fire took off, and he straggled down to the fish traps, undergarments in hand.

He washed his clothes and hung them on brush to dry, then snuck a few minutes to rock hunt. He selected rock after rock, shoved the keepers in his pockets, and tossed the culls back into the creek. Not expecting fish to be swimming circles in their heart-shaped boundaries, he sat down in the sand, shed his socks and boots, and rolled up his pant legs. He gawked at the trees across the creek as the sun's scarce rays warmed his face.

His stomach clenched with hunger. His feet slipped into cold water and he bit his lip as he braced against it. He meandered over slimy rocks and a swift current that slapped at his legs as he made his way to the first trap. He peered into the stick barriers, hands in his pockets, eyes wide as they caught movement. He froze in place. *Is my mind playin' tricks on me?*

He turned and glanced at the campsite.

Ross sat on a log by the fire, face in his hands.

Jed hadn't moved in hours.

"Hey! Over here." Delbert splashed toward the shore as if the sound would reach his friend. "Ross, look." His voice cracked with excitement as he tripped over a slimy rock and fell into the fish trap crushing the sticks. The fish darted out and swam downstream as if a bear was closing in. Alarm twisted his face. *Stupid boy.* The haunting voice surfaced. Woke up out of hibernation. He shooed it back into the cave with four simple words, "I will do this."

Yet he refused to look in Ross's direction. He knew

87

his friend would take every moment to torment him. He wiped his face with the back of his hand and stood in ankle deep water. The cold made him shiver while frustration raged inside. *I will do this.*

He decided to check the other traps. "One. Just one measly fish is all I want."

Delbert pitched forward as the current slapped against the back of his legs. He threw his arms to his sides and caught his balance. Still teetering against the current and slick stones under his feet, he bit his lips. His feet ached as they pounded on hard rocks, but he soldiered on. One foot in front of the other.

He stood beside the empty second trap. His stomach protested as his fists pumped in frustration. "I'm not gonna give up. Not this time. The others depend on me and I won't fail them."

Three more traps.

He moved on to the third. *Goose egg.* The fourth, none. He looked up to the heavens and prayed, "Lord, please. What will it take? We're starving, cold, hurt and tired. I need your favor. We need you to provide some kind of meal for us." He closed his eyes as if magically fish would appear. "Amen," he added.

He opened his eyes, looked straight into the trap, and fell down. This time he missed the sticks poking out of the sand. He came up hollering, "Ross, we got one."

Delbert slipped again and slammed back into the creek as the stream carried him further away from his food. He swam against the current and made his way to the trap. He gathered his balance and gave camp a sideways glance. A confused expression plastered Ross's face. But a look of almost-ready-to-barf washed it away.

Delbert snatched up the fish and held it high above his head. Ross clutched his belly and ran for the bushes. "Oops." Delbert chuckled. "Too soon, I reckon. Heck, serves the buzzard right."

Delbert toted his catch to the fire, chest puffed out, and set it down on one of the rocks. Drops of water sizzled and bounced off the hot surface. He patted his pocket, searching for his knife. His gut formed a sinking feeling as he snapped his head in the direction of the creek.

He shuffled a few steps toward the creek in heavy, soaked pants and halted. Searching the ground with bare toes, he uncovered leaves and rocks until he remembered sliding his knife into his cowboy boot. He plodded to the bank, collected his socks and boots, and made his way back to the fire, pants dripping. Pinecones and other debris that clung to his wet feet made for slow going. He sat on a log, brushed each foot clean, and checked his boots for the missing knife.

He stared at the single fish. "How will this feed us? That and a handful of berries." *Stupi...* "No!" he shouted.

Jed poked his head out of the tent. "What are you hollerin' about?"

Delbert stared at his dirt covered feet. "Nothin'."

"Uh-huh." Jed rubbed his brow and yawned. He stretched his arms up and dropped them as if rocks were tied around his wrists. He asked, "What's cookin'?"

Delbert held up the single fish. "This is."

"Just one? Is there more?"

"This's it."

"Okay." He paused. "That'll have to do. I'm not

89

complainin'. Anything else?" His gaze hopeful, he sniffed the air.

"How about those?" Delbert pointed to the pouch.

"Well…what's in it?"

"Berries. Juicy berries." Delbert poured out some in the palm of his hand and offered them to Jed. "Here. Have a sample."

Jed popped some into his open mouth. His jaw felt as if it were exploding with delight as he chewed. A grin formed on his lips and exposed blue teeth.

"I'll clean and cook this fish. Then we can eat."

Jed inched out of the tent.

"I'll help you, hold on." Delbert offered.

Jed put up his hand. "I got it."

"Gotta prove yourself, huh?" Familiar words rolled off Delbert's tongue.

"Yep." Jed inched toward the fire until he found a suitable spot. He bit his bottom lip as he moved. He rested. Inched closer. Rested. Looked around. "Hey, where's Ross?"

Delbert chortled. "He ate some poisonous berries. He's over in the bushes."

Jed chuckled. "Sick again? He's a hard learner. The most bull-headed fella I ever laid eyes on, that's for sure."

Delbert had the fish hissing by the time Ross showed his pale face. "Think you can eat?" he asked, sarcasm lathered his tone.

Ross sat down in the dirt by the fire. He leaned against the log and pulled his knees to his chest. "Not sure. Hate to squander such a hard won meal." His face pale. Puffy eye lids. Hair stuck out in all directions. Damp shirt pulled out. "Bet it took ya hours to pull this one in."

Delbert looked at Jed, but said nothing.

Jed scooted on his backside to the fire and leaned against a log. He sniffed the air and coughed. "The smell of cooked fish and puke isn't temptin' my appetite. We should just split this one, Del. Don't look like pale-face is up to eatin'."

Ross glared at him.

Jed shifted to straighten out his leg. "What?"

Ross groaned and slumped against a log. "We wouldn't be here if Delbert didn't have to keep some childish birthday promise." He closed his eyes. "All he's doing is trying to prove himself to his pa. He don't much care about us."

Delbert slammed the fish down and walked over to Ross. "You lazy, good for nothin' buzzard. I oughta—"

"Hey, Ross, still have some roots in your pouch?" Jed asked. "No need to start a war. We still haveta get home, right?"

Ross leaned forward, fist up.

"Hey, Ross. Did ya hear me?" Jed asked, leaning forward.

Ross looked at Jed and sank back against the log. "I think so. Go ahead and check." His upper lip curled.

Delbert walked off. He fumbled around in Ross's tent and found the pouch. He loosened the leather thong and peered in. "I'll be. The buzzard has roots and berries. I bet he's been hiding them all along."

Stiff legged, he brought the provisions out to show the others.

Ross turned his head. "My stomach's doin' flip-flops

'cause of that stinkin' fish."

Delbert tossed the pouch in Ross's lap. "Here's your food. Think you can handle it?"

Jed licked his lips. "Fresh food. I'll eat whatever you serve me." He rubbed his hands together and looked from Delbert to Ross. "You two better make peace. I'd like to get outta here alive."

Delbert nodded. His muscles relaxed. "Ross, try a sip first." Delbert handed him a cup of water. He was tempted to throw it in his face.

Ross put his lips to the edge and took a small sip. He eyeballed Delbert.

Delbert dished up three scant servings and sat down on a stump. He gave a silent prayer of thanks and dug in. He pulled out his pamphlet on rocks and thumbed through its pages. He studied the pictures and tried to memorize each scientific name of the minerals, a way to relax before another round of chores.

He tried to enjoy what he was reading, but the mental list they depended on for survival intruded: food, shelter, wood, food. His pa's words hounded him like a neglected toddler. "You need to learn these skills, son, and take them serious. Never know when you'll need 'em." He knew what needed to be done: chop firewood, store water, hunt for food. First on his list was to set a snare or two. He also needed to gather worms and grasshoppers for fish bait. The list poked at him long enough, so he tucked his pamphlet back into his pack and began his chores.

He looked his pals over. "I'll be back. Gonna go wrangle me some bait." He grunted as he walked past.

Ross's uneaten food on the ground caught Delbert's

eye. "You didn't eat much," he said. With pale face and saggy eyelids, Ross didn't look up when Delbert addressed him.

Delbert and Jed exchanged worried glances.

Delbert grabbed the fish, tore it in two, and lobbed one half to Jed. "Can't afford to waste."

Ross shrugged.

Delbert turned and walked into the woods.

CHAPTER 10

Dusk surrounded the camp as Delbert finished stacking the last chunk of wood on the pile. Thunder boomed in the distance. Seconds later a flash of lightening clawed at the heavens and cast dark shadows that ripped through the skyline. The horses stomped and whinnied as if crying out for protection.

Delbert counted, drawing out each number: *one, two, three, four, five…boom!* He gazed up at the dim treetops still visible, but fading fast.

Jed sniffed the air. "A storm's a comin'. And it's mighty angry." He shifted his weight and stared upward. "We need to make our way to higher ground…the cliff over there." He motioned to his right. "Hurry!"

Delbert shook his head. "You can't make it that far. We need to stay here. I'll move our tents under those fir trees"—he pointed to his left—"the ones with long swooping branches. Stake 'em tight. There's enough of a slant the rain will drain off and right into the creek." Torn apart fish traps entered into Delbert's mind long enough to ignite worry. *God, help us.* A raindrop tickled his nose. "It's here, boys," he said.

Ross sneered at Delbert. "I think we know what fir

branches look like."

"Ross, can ya help me?" Jed asked.

He looked like a cat beaten by a dog in a water trough, but he nodded. "I think so." Ross pushed to his feet. Delbert watched him sway.

"Del, help!" Jed crumpled to the ground.

Delbert sprinted to Ross's side. "You all right?"

Ross moaned and reached for his head. He curled into a fetal position.

"Hold still. I'll move the tents real quick and come back for you guys. Jed, stoke the fire. We'll need the coals."

Jed nodded and inched his way to the nearby woodpile. He tossed on a log and sent sparks into the sky. Pitch sizzled and smoked. He leaned over and took hold of another small piece of wood. It too sparked and smoked after he lobbed it on. It rolled off and came to rest on the side of the fire. He frowned. "I'm not so much help, am I?" He clutched a third bit of tamarack and flung it, eyed the flames as a marksman does his target. The log landed in the middle and shot flames in tangled directions. Jed smiled and sat taller.

"You're help enough," Delbert said.

Ross crawled to a tree, held onto a branch near the trunk, and stood.

Jed turned his attention to his friend just in time to see the boy scramble for the bushes.

"Delbert," Jed said, he motioned over his shoulder.

"I see him." Delbert said as he dragged a tent full of contents toward the fir trees.

"Hey, look at me." Jed leaned toward Delbert.

Delbert stopped, stood straight, hands on his sides. "What?" His tone dripped with irritation.

"Do you think Ross is gonna be okay?"

Delbert scanned the area. "Where is he?"

"Bushes."

"Uh-huh. Food poisoning takes a spell to get out of your system. He'll manage." Delbert continued to tug and drag the tent over rocks, sticks, and other debris.

By the time the tents were relocated, the drizzle turned into a sideways-rain-slapping downpour that stung their eyes. Ross stumbled back to camp and settled under his blanket. The pelts of rain against canvas muffled his moans.

"You almost done? I'm gettin' soaked here." Jed brushed soggy bangs out of his face. The fire almost out, he shivered so hard his teeth chattered. "My muscles sure do ache." He started to scoot uphill when Delbert stopped him. "Here. Let me help you up. Grab onto this."

Delbert held a forked branch in front of Jed. Jed grasped it. Delbert clutched Jed under his arm and heaved him up. Jed hopped a few steps in order to gain his balance. He towered over his help.

Jed admired his crutch. "Where'd you git this? And when?"

"I found it this morning while I collected twigs and moss for the fire."

"Why didn't you give it to me?"

"Your ankle needs the rest. I figured you'd try hobbling all over the place with it."

"I'm no tenderfoot." Jed blinked against the rain. "But you could be right."

Delbert and Jed limped up the incline of slick grass. They slipped a few times, but reached Jed's tent. He scooted under his blanket, damp clothes and all, and settled in for the night. Eye lids heavy, he yawned. "I'm so tired. Hope my mind settles down so I can get some shut-eye. I need sleep."

Delbert pulled a hunk of willow bark out of his pocket. "Here. Chew on this."

Jed grabbed the bark and chewed. Let the saliva build up before swallowing.

Delbert rushed around, gathered large rocks, and placed them in the dirt forming a circle. He searched the ground and focused on a yellow flower with large, wet leaves. He plucked several soft leaves off and hurried to the fire. Under the half burnt logs Jed placed on earlier, red coals glowed, just as he hoped. He found two branches and lifted the coals from the pit onto the leaves. He dashed to the new fire pit and dropped the crimson fireballs into the dirt. Heat penetrated the leaves but didn't burn his fingers. He placed black and green moss he'd gleaned earlier that day on the coals. "I'm glad to have these. Never expected such a storm."

Delbert squatted down to protect the coals, and blew with the force of a hand-held fan. He blinked against smoke swirling up and in his face, wiped tears away as he slid right. The smoke followed him so he moved again. The smoke drifted and encircled his body. Delbert rubbed his eyes and blinked away tears. Instead of dancing with smoke any longer, he gathered more sticks for flames that struggled to keep alive. "We need more dry fuel."

Wet wood stacked by the old fire pit caught his attention. He set the top pieces aside and gathered the dry ones. He drummed up a few pinecones. "Ouch!" He looked at the orb of blood on his finger and picked out the tip of a pinecone scale with his teeth. Once he'd inspected the piece of cone scale that resemble the stinger of a wasp, he spit it into the fire. He rubbed his hands on his pant leg. It hurt and he held back curse words. Cupped hands, he blew which created thicker, gray smoke. But this time he blew with force. His eyes squeezed shut and now holding his breath, he let the tears flow, blindly adding a handful of moss, twigs, and dry pine needles. "Hope I'm hittin' the mark," he said.

He couldn't hold his breath any longer and had to walk away. He drew in clean, damp air into his burning lungs. He swiped his face with a soggy sleeve and noticed the black stain. The smell of ash filled his nose. Rain washed away the sting in his eyes as he held his face up and let the drops run over him.

He peered into a tent and watched Ross's motionless, limp body. Worry for his friend twisted his gut with each passing minute. "Maybe Jed was right. We should've paid better attention to you." But for now all he could do was hunker down under the protection of the fir branches and wait out the storm.

The sharp *whack, whack* of chopped kindling bounced off the rain. He stoked the now popping fire. Heat dried his skin and it began to itch. His clothes steamed. He found a spot to sit close to the heat and put his hands out, but not too close to scorch them or his clothes. Native legends swirled in his head and stopped on the story of how fire was started. Pekam shared this and other stories with Delbert throughout the years.

Male elders in Pekam's village told coyote legends through winter months as women sewed by firelight.

99

Delbert sat and stared into flames as blue and yellow hues jigged, chewing on damp fuel.

He decided to tell the fire legend, aloud, in case Jed and Ross were still awake. If not he would repeat it in the morning. He would at least keep himself company as his mind wound up, not allowing for sleep.

In the distance he heard horses stomp and paw the ground. "They haven't been watered all day." A sick feeling came over him. He rushed over, untied them, and walked agitated horses to the creek. He rubbed their necks. "Sorry, boys. We'd better pay closer attention to ya." He stroked Charlie's back. He fumbled in his pocket for a treat. There were none.

The horses snorted as water dripped from their lips and soon went back for more. Over and over they dipped their heads until they'd tanked up. They pawed at the cool water and splashed themselves. Delbert as well. He knew they were done and led them to a grassy patch, hobbling their legs with thick strips of latigo. The wind whipped, hurling rain sideways.

Delbert scurried back to the fire and covered himself with a wool blanket. The fire sizzled and hissed. Smoke spiraled fingers upward. He felt relief, knowing the fir trees hovered above his head and provided enough shelter from the elements. "All I need to do is keep this fire roarin'," he said and tossed a few more pinecones on the heap.

His thoughts drifted back to Pekam's story.

"Not sure if you boys are awake, but I'm gonna tell you about the Sinyekst legend of the origin of fire." He imagined himself teaching eager students.

He heard Jed snicker. Lightening again streaked the

sky followed by the *boom* of thunder.

He glanced in the direction of the horses. Hooves pounded the ground before they settled down to graze. *Sure glad I didn't put 'em back on the picket line. At least now they can move a little and not feel trapped.*

Delbert waited for thunder to pass. He straightened his spine and stretched his stiff back muscles.

"One day, long ago, it rained so long and so hard all the fires on earth extinguished." He spoke over the rain. "The animals held a council meeting and decided to make war against the sky in order to bring back fire. It was essential for cooking and the animals were not about to back down. They were warriors, not whelps.

"The animals waited for spring to show its face. Excitement electrified the village. Arrows were gathered and nocked onto bowstrings and let loose into the brilliant blue sky. The arrows soared high, but to no avail. In fact, all had failed. Coyote stepped up and plucked his bowstring carved out of western yew. 'Nice and tight,' he said and squinted. He yanked an arrow out of the quiver strapped to his back and secured the arrow noch to the string.

"He pulled his arm back, aimed, and released the arrow. It flew high, but not high enough. It arched and landed back on the dry, dusty earth. It was Chickadee's turn. He rustled the dust off his feathers and pulled an arrow out of his small quiver. He fingered the arrow and stared up to the sky, concentration etched in his face. He retrieved his bow and strummed the string to make sure it was taut. When satisfied, he nocked the arrow to the string and pulled back. He wiggled his tail feathers and shivers crawled up his neck. He steadied his stance and locked his attention on the target before letting the arrow

101

fly. His arrow swung high and reached the sky. He continued to shoot arrow after arrow, forming a chain that allowed the rest of the animals to climb up.

"The last one to lumber up was Grizzly Bear. The arrows creaked under his bulky weight and finally one broke off. He was stuck, not able to join the others. A look of shock spread over his face and a tear trickled down his furry cheek.

"The animals glanced back with sorrowful looks on their faces. They felt sorry for Grizzly Bear, but knew they had to push on. They were warriors in a fight for survival. Grizzly Bear clung to the arrow, disappointed he couldn't help."

Delbert stoked the fire. He heard Jed stir in his tent, but wasn't sure if he was awake or not. He glanced over at Ross's tent and saw no movement. Delbert cleared his throat, took a sip out of his cup, spit out flakes of ash, and continued.

"When the animals reached the sky, they found themselves in a lush green valley near a sparkling lake filled with wildflowers. They stood quietly and drank in its beauty. The people of the sky fished off the shore as they talked, and laughed. Coyote wished to act as a scout,"— Delbert's voice grew louder with each word—"but his vying for leadership resounded off the hills and the people of the sky snuck up behind him. He was taken captive.

"Muskrat peered around as he hid behind brush, quiet as a mouse. He dug holes along the shore of the lake while Beaver and Eagle set out to capture the fire. Beaver forged a plan. He snuck into one of the fish traps and pretended to be dead. The people of the sky carried him to the chief's house and began to skin Beaver.

Luckily Eagle swooped in and landed on a tree near the tent. When the people of the sky saw Eagle, they ran out. At once Beaver snatched a clamshell full of glowing coals and ran away."

Delbert swallowed another sip of water, listened for movement from the boys, and clinked the cup down on a rock.

"He jumped into the lake. The people tried to catch him in nets, but Beaver was too swift. The water now drained through the holes Muskrat made. There was no way the people of the sky could catch the animals now."

Delbert tossed more kindling on the fire. It formed a tipi-type structure that let air into the fire. The flames licked at the wood and the rain droplets sizzled as they bounced off hot rocks. Delbert slid the blanket off his shoulders and placed it beside him. The fire now warmed him. The downpour slowed to a sprinkle.

"The animals ran back to the chain made of Chickadee's arrows. They came to a screeching halt and found all of the arrows broken. So each bird gave a ride to the rest of the animals and flew them back to the ground. Coyote and Sucker were left in the sky, so Coyote tied a piece of buffalo robe to each paw and jumped down. He rode on the hide, sailed downward, and landed on the branches of a pine tree—a nice soft landing.

"The following morning, Coyote showed off his wings made out of buffalo hide. He tried to shrug them off, but they stuck and transformed him into a bat. Sucker jumped down and shattered his bones. The animals fitted his bones together, but some came up missing, so they put pine needles into his tail instead. Therefore, Sucker has many bones."

103

He paused.

Jed clapped a little too loud, splitting the silence of the forest. "Fine story, Del."

A feeling of appreciation sprang up inside of him. "How's your ankle? Need some more willow bark to chew on?"

"Nah, I'm all right. Now that you're done telling stories, I'm lookin' for some shut-eye."

Delbert laughed. "I'll stay up for a spell. Keep the fire burnin'."

He put one last log on the fire and leaned against a tree trunk. He covered up with his damp wool blanket and pulled out his pamphlet. "I'd best stay by the fire so Coyote don't slither in and try to steal it."

CHAPTER 11

July 20, 1867
Day Six

Delbert awoke shivering, soaked, and hungrier than ever. His stomach felt hollow, his legs weak. The fire had long been out. Birds sang joyous tunes as they fluttered damp wings. He rubbed his eyes and sat up. The wet blanket felt heavy on his legs so he pitched it over a log. He gazed at his empty tent and groaned. "I wish I'd been savvy enough to sleep in it."

Steam rose off dew-covered grass as the sun heated the morning air. It smelled fresh. The warmth from his blanket enticed him to stay put, but he pulled himself up and staggered around. He found some moss and tugged it off the trees. It felt dry. He uncovered somewhat dry wood from underneath a top layer of the soaked branch pile. He tossed what he could in the soggy fire pit and fished his rock and flint piece out of his pocket.

"I shoulda stayed awake."

He struck the rock on the flint and sparks flew, but none took hold. He yawned and rubbed his face with dirty hands before striking the flint again. "Ow!" he yelled. His thumb turned red, the size of a small rock. He bit his lip against the pain and cradled his thumb.

With blood trickling, he picked up the flint rock and attempted a third strike. This time sparks ignited and a small stream of smoke wove its way around moss and pine needles. Hope swirled around his muscles as they began to relax. A small flame poked its head out, hungry, begging for more fuel. Delbert felt if he didn't get substantial food soon, he and the boys would share the same fate as the flame struggling to survive.

He hunkered down, leaned closer, and blew a whisper of air, just enough to breathe life into the tiny orange flicker. He tucked a smidgen of moss under the pine needles and blew one more time. The flames spit and popped as they ate through their meal. The heat felt good as he rubbed his hands close to the flames.

He chopped kindling, changed into dry clothing, and hung his wet ones over logs. All he had to do is remember to pick them up and toss them into his tent once dry. He made his way to the shoreline where despair came over him like last night's rainstorm. He sat down and cupped his face. "Lord, I'm trying to trust you, but it seems harder when nothing's going our way," he said, looking up. "Pa taught me to pray and trust, so I reckon I'd better, even if it takes time for the answer to come. But I'm tired. Worn to the size of an ant. I guess like Ma says, 'The Lord's timing is always perfect.' Reckon I'll try a little harder. It's tough when fella's like us are so hungry." He looked up.

Delbert knelt by the creek and watched the current slither by. Uncertainty slid into his mind. *What are we gonna do? Will we die out here? Will anyone find our decaying bodies?*

He pulled his boots and socks off. Despair sank further into his soul and crushed his chest. He wasn't looking forward to dipping his already cold feet into the frigid water. He sat for a spell. *I could set more snares instead.* He pondered that idea. *Checking traps may put an arrow or two in my quiver.* He snatched a rock from the bank and turned it in his palm. *Ross has better luck with snares.*

A shiver coursed through his soggy veins. His stomach tightened and twisted, reminding him of its emptiness. *Not sure if I can push through this raging current.*

"Enough already." He sucked in his hollow gut, clenched his teeth, and tiptoed in. He felt like he should check to see if a yellow streak ran down his backside. It would fit his mood. He sucked in a breath and turned around to see if the others were awake and snickering. No sign of life. He released the breath.

Delbert made his way to the first trap. Sure as shootin', a fish swam in its parameters. "Pa's right! Timing's everything."

He scooped the fish into his hands and flung it on the bank. It flopped in the air and landed with the *thud*. He darted over to make sure the fish wouldn't flop back into the creek. With determination, he dug a hole in the dirt, splashed water into the pit, and filled it up. He tossed his catch into its holding pen and dashed back in, not bothered by the creek's icy fingers pricking at his ankles.

Trap number two. A second fish swirled about—a red-bellied trout. He whooped and hollered this time, not caring if he woke his pals. "Boys, get up! Lookee here. Come on now, let's get goin'." Delbert clutched the fish so tight it almost slipped out of his grasp. He pulled it to his chest and cradled it like a newborn baby. He dropped that one in the holding pen and went back for more.

Ross slipped out of his tent and rubbed his sore belly. He used his hand to block the sun and squinted to see the commotion through hazy vision.

Jed wiggled and waved the sides of his tent. He poked his head out and shaded his eyes from the sun's rays that peered from behind dark clouds. "What's goin' on?"

"Delbert's down there, excited about somethin'. Don't know." Ross searched for his cup, his mouth so dry his voice came out sounding like a sick elk trying to bugle. He stretched and rubbed his stiff neck.

Jed scooted out of his tent, dragging his make-shift crutch. "Where's the willow bark?" he asked Ross. A pleading look spanned his face. "Not sure what's burning more, my gut or my ankle. How do you feel this morning?"

"Not sure. But *my* gut's a ton better." Ross fled for the bushes as nature called. He shuffled back and sat by the fire. His hands and feet began to thaw. He and Jed watched Delbert jump into the creek, drag himself to the next fish trap, and dance around as he scooped up a fish and brought it back to the holding hole.

Ross stoked the fire a time or two. "I wonder if I should go and help 'im?"

"Nah. Look at him. He's having so much fun. This is good for him. Makes 'im feel more confident." Jed laughed as Delbert hopped in and out of the creek. He danced and cheered. Even Ross's grumpy frown turned up and formed a smile—small as it was.

"Wanna find me some willow bark? My ankle's killin' me."

"Sure. I can do that."

"Now?"

"Yeah." Ross forced his gaze from Delbert to Jed.

He saw the pain twist his friend's face and jumped to his feet. "You need more bark juice." He retrieved a chunk of willow bark from Delbert's doeskin pack and filled a cup with water. The birds chirped and flapped and kept his attention until he remembered he had cold water in his hand. He placed the cup by the fire to boil and sliced some bark off and plopped it in the cup. Water splashed out and sizzled on the rocks, so he added more. He held out a sliver for Jed to chew on. A bird sang. Silence. A second answered. Ross's mom always sang with birds at their cabin. Tears pooled and he shook his head.

Jed cleared his throat. "I got it from here. You go and help the great fisherman." He leaned back, gritted his teeth.

"Yeah, I gotta see what he's up to." Ross jogged down to the bank and peered into the hole Delbert dug. He whooped and held up his hands.

Jed leaned forward. "How many?"

"Five. No six of 'em."

Delbert looked up from the fifth trap and shouted back. His arms snapped into the air. The voices of all three boys bounced off the rock cliffs and sent echoes deep into the woods. Delbert scooped up another fish. He cradled it back to the shore. "That's the last one."

109

"You did it," Ross bellowed.

Hands raised in victory, Delbert said, "Yeah. Sure did."

"I think he's figuring himself out," Ross said.

Jed nodded. "You hit the mark with the arrow on that one."

Delbert cleaned the fish and sat down by the fire. He and Ross roasted the trout. It didn't take long to gobble the fish and wash it down with gulps of water. But the fullness didn't last long. And there were no berries for added flavor. No fruit. No fresh vegetables out of anyone's garden. No homemade peach cobbler. Delbert's belly rumbled as the fish teased his hunger. He looked at his friends; their hopeless expressions told the same story.

He sat at the fire and watched Jed and Ross, the corners of their mouths turned down. Their once sparkling eyes now dull as they stared into the dimming flames.

Delbert swirled coals with a stick. *Now what?*

"Need more bait," Delbert stated. He gazed up at the blueberry colored sky. "Don't have much time."

"I can set more snares." Ross's attention darted between the two like a hummingbird flitting from flower to flower, sucking nectar.

Jed sipped the blood-red willow bark tea. "What can I do?"

"Quit frettin' for starters," Delbert replied with a playful smile. "Keep the fire going and rest your ankle.

110

We'll need you later."

Jed grunted his consent. "Reckon that'll have to do." He tossed small pieces of wood on the glowing coals and watched them ignite.

CHAPTER 12

Ross wandered around the woods by himself in search of tracks. Squirrel tracks. Chipmunk tracks. Heck, even mouse tracks. He narrowed his eyes and crouched low to the ground to study a few small prints in front of him. "No squirrel here."

He knew squirrel tracks displayed long hind feet with five toes and lots of pads while short front feet showed four toes and a few pads.

He brushed away some leaves. "No tiny claw marks indented into the soaked earth." A puzzled look crossed his face. "Not a chipmunk. Not a mouse. Four toes and a bit bigger." Ross studied the lopsided prints. "A paw print perhaps lifted up? The animal seems to be hopping on three legs. Maybe wounded? A small dog or pup? But as a single set of prints, it couldn't be a pup. No mother's tracks beside it. And too small to be an adult." He spoke in a low tone.

Ross rubbed his chin. He searched the forest floor in hope of finding broken branches, a nest, bedded down grass, some sort of clue. He was east and about an hour away from camp in a nice wooded area close to the creek. He felt relief having time to himself. And he was in the

113

perfect place to hunt small game, knowing fresh meat wouldn't make him puke. He decided to move on.

He paced several steps, stopped, and crouched low, a single knee to the ground. He brushed aside some leaves and twigs and noticed teardrop shaped deer hooves. "Fresh venison. Our hunger problems would be over." He paused. "One problem: no rifle. No bow and arrow. Not even a spear."

His belly rumbled. He wiped his dry mouth with his sleeve as if a drop of saliva escaped his lips. He laughed at his unconscious movement. What he really wanted to do was cry. Studying the tracks he said, "I could make a spear, but I'm not fast enough to run a swift beast like that down. Maybe if there were a few of them, or us, but still. Expert hunters can manage such a feat, not sure gangly, half-grown men can. Half-starved at that." The sound of breaking twigs caught his attention. He listened and determined it was some small critter like a chipmunk or squirrel.

Ross realized such daydreams would not fill his empty belly. Once the sound faded, he went back to the task at hand. He had to set as many snares as he could and fast. He trudged further down the trail on legs that swayed like the tops of larch trees in a windstorm.

He continued to scan the ground and soon came across additional tracks. Hope stirred inside as he stopped to get a closer look. His focus locked on long prints.

He knelt down and his hand swept leaves and twigs aside which revealed a perfect set of rabbit tracks. Hind feet set wider than the front, a sure hopping sign. He dropped his pouch, drew out twine, and rummaged through the pack a second time. He found the right-sized stick and another with a perfect Y-shape. Ross could smell the meat rotating over the fire, see its juices dribbling and sizzling in orange and blue, hungry flames.

His trembling fingers made a loop with twine and fastened it to thin sticks. He set the snares as Pekam instructed him by staking them at the edge of the trail, low to the ground. He worked with haste, finding several tracks within feet of one another and swelled with a feeling of hope and pride. He set five snares. More tracks headed east, but he was out of twine. There was no vegetation in sight to braid more rope.

"Pine needles're too short. Vines grow in the lower regions and can't even be harvested till fall. Same with cattails. Let's see…"

A red-tailed hawk cried in the distance. Ross's gaze shifted upward. The hawk spiraled down and lifted up again. The bird sailed for a time and finally glided to the tip of a larch tree. His talons wrapped around a branch. Huge feathers rustled as the hawk settled in for a rest. "You must be hunting. Well, leave my critters alone now, ya hear, *Pia*?" Recalling the Sinyekst name Pekam gave to Delbert a few years back in a ceremony of honor made Ross smile. Secretly he wished Pekam would give him a name. Something like Fierce Grizzly would do just fine.

Ross gathered up his pack and headed back to camp. He was outright curious how the fish traps were doing. He hoped more rabbits would end up in the snares than trout in Delbert's fish traps.

He whistled as he walked, chest puffed up like his uncle's prized rooster parading around the ranch. A pinecone flew into the air after making contact with the toe of his boot. Feeling as spry as he was, Ross scooped up a dead branch, peeled what remaining limbs were left and swung it around like a man at war.

115

Pretending Delbert and Jed were with him he said, "I'll show ya this old trick, Delbert boy. Get on up, now, Jed. Don't be bashful, boys. Fight like a man—a warrior." Ross tripped and fell. He jumped up with stick in hand and fought the air again. He danced around with caked mud on his boots. It was thicker than before. His verbal jabs increased in volume with each jumbled step. Echoes cracked through the stillness of the forest as he goaded Delbert and Jed as if surrounding him.

He swung that old branch to the right, twisting his wrist to bring it back to the left, and swung the branch up as if reaching for the clouds. He swung hard and high and twirled around. The tip of the branch landed hard on a wasp hive and it burst forth, producing an army of buzzing, angry creatures. Ross threw the stick aside and ran. He tripped and rolled as wasps engulfed his head and neck, flailing like a bear on fire. He kept rolling in hope of squashing some of the irate insects.

His skin stung as if a hundred tiny needles jabbed him. No one heard his cries for help. He rolled to his feet, ran for the creek, and jumped in. He counted to twenty and shot out of the water. His lungs felt like they were on fire. He gasped for air. Fingers clamped around his throat, he bent over to catch his breath.

"I hate wasps!" Ross slowly stood. He looked around and watched for the tiny devils. Didn't hear buzzing. "Best be gone, you demons." He thought about what the Sinyekst kids were yelling at them when they'd left the village. Where there evil spirits lurking in the trees? Did they send wasps to chase him and the boys away?

He scratched his face. It felt as though his flesh sizzled, like frying bacon, and it spread across his face. He plunged deep into the water, holding himself in until he

116

thought he'd pass out. His body red and numb, he stumbled out with blurred vision. He grimaced from pain and clawed at the burn. His vision hazy, he tried to open his eyes wider, but heavy lids prevented him. They felt as if ten pounds of mud caked them. Gentle fingers explored his swollen lids and face, and he sank to the ground.

His thoughts reeled with fear. *What if I go blind? How'll I get back to the others? How will I check my snares?*

He heard the red-tailed hawk squawk and knew the beast laughed at him. His neck, chest, and face burned so he crawled back to the creek and again dunked his head under. He sat back on his feet and lifted his face toward the heavens. "Lord, you have to get me back!" His stomach clenched as panic set in. Sweat broke out and dripped down his back. His body trembled.

At least he could breathe, a favorable sign.

Delbert gave up on catching crickets as it was late in the morning. "They're mighty quick today. Or I'm too weak. I seem to have lost my get-up-and-go," he said walking past Jed.

Sweat ran down his neck and back. He stumbled to the creek, dropped to his knees, and slurped handfuls of water. But too fast. "Ow! My head!" He moaned as he slammed his head into his hands, rocking back and forth.

He heard Jed chuckle as his friend watched from the bank. He tended the fire while sipping his willow bark tea.

When the jabbing pain in Delbert's head eased, he rolled onto his back and pulled off damp boots and socks. The smell made him gag. His feet were blistered and sore. He rolled up his pants and stood, shoulders slumped, with a grimace plastered on his face. On this cool, gloomy day, the sound of the creek was not tempting.

However, hunger urged him to tiptoe in and check each fish trap. Water came up to his knees before he remembered to fetch worms left on the bank. *Hunger must be affectin' my memory.* He jabbed each worm with the end of the pointed stick and plunged the tip and the struggling worm into the creek bed.

He gave a sideways glance to Jed, who lifted his cup in the air. *Humph.* He pretended not to notice, sure Jed's gesture was meant to rib and not offend. He snuck one last look at the fish trap before heading back to camp.

He said a little prayer before trudging to the fire. He drug his toes in the dirt. Took small steps, head down. At this point, his feet were numb. He plunked down on a stump and warmed his red limbs close to the flames, but not to close. Heat from the fire warmed his britches and steam burned his legs, so he scooted back. He looked at his boots and socks. "I just want something in my stomach."

Jed snickered. "You look pathetic. My grandmother can walk faster than you. Come on over and share your troubles with me, brother." He held out his cup of bark juice.

Delbert plopped down on a log. "You don't know what you're—"

Delbert's heads snapped around when he heard what sounded like a wild hog screeching in the brush. Branches broke and feet pounded.

Jed twisted around, unable to get a good look. "What is it?"

Ross crashed through the trees, arms waving in the air as though on fire. "Wasps. Move. Wasps! I've been attacked."

Delbert jumped to his feet and ran toward Ross. Were wasps chasing him? Was he stung? How much? Would he die? The two collided. Ross thrown one way and Delbert another, both landed on their backs.

Jed ducked, and covered himself with his arms. "Why'd you bring them with you?"

Ross rolled from side to side. Blood smeared his face.

Delbert squeezed into a fetal position. In pain, he held his nose. "I think it's broken."

"Ross…Delbert…are you okay?" Jed sounded frantic. He searched the air. "What's the commotion about? There's no wasps. You find some bad plants out there?"

Ross scrambled to his feet and stumbled to the creek. He plunged in and allowed himself to drift downstream.

"Delbert! Get Ross. He's floatin' away."

Delbert rose to his knees. He clutched his head in his hands.

Jed braced against his crutch and attempted to stand.

"Sit down. I'll get 'im." Delbert eyed the creek. "You aren't going anywhere."

Jed plopped down and cried out in pain. "Get goin'." he said through clenched teeth.

Delbert raced to the creek, jumped in, and stretched his arms forward. He pulled them back as his body torpedoed faster down the current. His muscles tightened with each stroke as his arms moved like dual windmills in a hurricane. He tried to peer up and see how far away Ross was, but water blurred his vision. No luck. He tucked his chin and swam with all the strength he could muster.

After several hard strokes, Delbert's hand felt a body. He clutched Ross's shirt and hauled him to a fallen tree that hung over the creek like a fisherman with a salmon in his net. He tugged against the current, his jaw clenched tight. One last yank and grunt pulled Ross to Delbert.

Ross gasped for air.

Delbert clung to the slick tree branch. His hand cramped. As Ross began to slip out of Delbert's grip, he reached up and clung to Delbert's shirtsleeve and pulled himself close.

"Hang on," Delbert shouted.

Delbert griped the branch tighter, wrapping his cold, stiff fingers around its base. He tried to catch his breath. "You okay now?"

Ross nodded. He clung tight to Delbert's shirtsleeve, knuckles white. "How about you?"

Delbert nodded back. He leaned against the log and thanked his Creator for the lifeline.

Chapter 13

Delbert sat by the fire cold, hungry, and exhausted. As dusk approached, neither snare nor fish trap had been checked. Delbert peered at Jed who looked downtrodden. He turned to Ross, whose face scrunched in pain.

Delbert started to say something, but took one look at his pals and kept quiet. He touched the bruises on his face from when he'd slammed into Ross. A stiff neck and sore mouth didn't make him feel much better.

Ross's eyes almost swollen shut, his lips looked like two plump night crawlers attached themselves and settled in for the night. Red scratch marks sliced down his cheeks and neck.

Jed stared at blue and orange flames. "The scent of larch reminds me of home. I miss it."

Delbert sighed. "Yeah."

"Owooee!" Ross howled in frustration. The vibrating noise coming out of his mouth sounded like a building storm. He scratched his hot, stinging flesh.

"You need something wet and cool on your face?" Delbert's tone took on an air of defeat.

"Sure do. There's a shirt in my tent."

Delbert pulled out the ragged shirt and carried it to the creek. He swirled it around and eyed the traps. Curiosity pulled him toward the creek. He wrapped the cool shirt around his neck and trudged out to them. He checked the left trap. *Empty.* He dug against the current and made his way to the other side. *Nothing.* Anger fueled his body as he traipsed from trap to vacant trap.

He pulled the shirt from his neck, swirled it around in the creek, and marched back to the fire. "This is as foolish as huntin' with a grass arrow. We should've never come"—Delbert jabbed his finger to the heavens—"I should've listened to my gut. What a mistake. We're starving to death." Delbert kicked the dirt and it sprayed into the fire. Sparks spiraled out.

"Settle down, Del." Jed ducked to the left, tipping over and landing on his side. Color drained from his face as he grimaced in renewed pain.

"Hey!" A piece of red ember as hot as Delbert's temper landed in Ross's lap. He jumped up and brushed coal away. He stood, a hint of blue peeking through engorged lids. He looked like he wanted to punch Delbert in the face. His fists pumped the air. A vein in his neck pulsed.

Delbert froze. He looked at Ross's miserable expression and turned to Jed's twisted gaze. His stare dropped to his mud-caked boots. "Look at the mess I've gotten us all into. Coincidence? Hah. Stupidity? Right on target. My arrows come up short when attempting to stick real food, but always seem to hit the bull's eye when the target's my own recklessness."

Jed looked at him, not knowing what to say.

Ross held out his hand for the shirt.

"Sorry. I…" He couldn't find words to justify his actions. He pounded his forehead.

Ross turned his attention to Jed and handed him more willow bark tea and poured some for himself. Ross scratched his face. Delbert noticed the soggy shirt in his fist and held it out.

Ross grunted. "Quit feeling sorry for yourself." He plucked the dripping shirt out of Delbert's hand without looking up.

Delbert walked off at a brisk clip. Not able to escape his shame, he felt his face flush. "Self-pity. Here I'm trying to apologize and that sidewinder just has to open his mouth. Let the venom loose. I swear…"

He marched toward the horses and walked like a predator—straight at them. They backed up, ears pricked ahead, and eyes wide. He untied them and stumbled down to the creek, fists pumping. The horses pulled against his rough grip and a struggle wiggled its way down the lead rope. Delbert yanked harder. The horses gave way and followed him, tension in the line.

The geldings hesitated to drink until Delbert knelt and swallowed water out of his cupped hands. Their gazes locked on him. Finally lowering their muzzles, they snorted then sucked in large amounts of water. Their ears swiveled in all directions, listening, alert.

Delbert's pulse quickened. "Sorry you've all been neglected." He thought of Pekam and Spupaleena. "They treat their mounts like they're some kinda royalty. None of us gave you boys a second glance today."

He tore off the corner of his shirt and dipped it in the water, wiping off his face and neck. "Sorry ol' boys." He spoke in a whisper. "We've been so selfish, worryin' about our own needs. Or at least I have. I've screwed up in more ways than one. The others have been busy gettin' themselves into a bit of trouble as well." He rubbed his gelding with apologetic strokes.

When the horses had their fill, he led them up the bank and rubbed them down with grass. He spoke to them in a soft tone, using slow, even strokes. He could feel their muscles soften to his touch. Heads dropped as they chewed. "Guess I'll stay here with you fellas for a spell. Time apart from the boys may be necessary for my survival. And theirs. Although I'm sure they're planning my death," he said to Charlie.

Delbert's hands warmed as he rubbed his gelding's hair. As his body relaxed, his mind wandered to Pekam's story about the fishing weir. His heart thumped in his chest as he focused on how the weir would have to be built—alone. "So, Charlie, do you think I can do it? Do I have the strength to cut and drag in all the poles I need. Will larch work, or do I need cottonwood?"

His palms sweat as the evil thoughts slipped back in: *Stupid boy, what are you thinking? You can't accomplish such a task. You have no skills. You are weak and tired and your belly is empty.*

"No! I *can* do this. I do have the skills. I have a knife and a hatchet. I know what to use and I know where the cottonwood trees are. I *am* strong enough. You can't lie to me anymore." He turned his attention to the geldings and rubbed as he talked. "I know I can do this. I'll have to find suitable twine. What can I use?" He looked down. "We wear boots, so no buckskin ties…" He searched the woods. "I can't harvest enough hemp, quality hemp for rope that is. Besides it's the wrong time of year. I've seen the women with Spupaleena harvest the hemp in the fall.

This is summer. What else?"

Charlie nudged him. "I hit a dandy spot, didn't I?" Delbert rubbed the bay's shoulder for a few extra moments as he allowed his mind to figure out each detail.

Stroking Charlie's neck, he continued, "We could shred one of the tents into thin strips and share the other two. I could make Jed and Ross split the blanket." He chuckled. "I'm sure they wouldn't mind." Delbert sidestepped a couple times. He worked his way down the horse's back. "They shouldn't put up much of a fight. Jed can hardly stand, let alone throw a punch. Ross's eyes are still swelled shut. He can't see well enough to hit a bull in the nose if it tried to charge him." Laughter escaped his lips as images of the battered pair reeled through his mind.

Delbert hummed as he massaged the horse. He moved from Charlie's head down toward his hindquarters. He fingered the length of the gelding's tail a few times like a comb, thinking back to an earlier time. "The braid wasn't strong enough before. We need something different. Not a single braid with three scrawny strands, but thick like a rope."

Delbert shoved his hands in his pockets and pulled them out. "Where did I put my knife?" He held his hands in front of him and said, "Stay boys," as if they were dogs. He sprinted back to camp.

"What's your hurry?" Jed asked.

"I have a plan." Delbert searched from log to Ross, to Jed, to the tent. "Where's my knife?"

Ross scoffed. "We're your caretakers now?"

"No, I just need it."

"Don't know. Where'd you have it last?" Jed scanned

the ground.

Delbert headed for his tent. He pulled his disheveled blanket off the dirt floor and shook it out. The knife clunked to the ground.

Ross scratched his face. "What are you up to?"

"I'll tell you when I know more…"

Delbert rushed by. He wanted to try and twist the hair into a cord while he could still see the black of the horse's tail in daylight.

Delbert turned back, slid the dry, warm shirt out of Ross's hands, ran it down to the creek and dunked it a few times. He saw the horses watching him flit around like a hungry bird, ears pinned forward, grass hanging out of their mouths. He rushed the sopping shirt back to Ross, shoved it in his hands, and returned to the gelding's backside.

He slid his knife out of the leather sheath and clutched a large hunk of Charlie's tail. The sheath dropped to the ground and Delbert flicked it to the side with the toe of his boot. Just as the knife was about to hack the chunk, Delbert pulled his hand away. He put his knife between his knees and twisted the hair around, exposing the back of it. "I best not hack off the front. Ma'll come after me with a switch." He clutched his fingers around the knife and see-sawed the blade through the hair until it broke loose, missing the skin of the tail.

He drew out a pinky-sized strand of leg-long hair and placed the remains on the ground. He fetched his knife and wiped the blade on his pant legs before slipping it in its cover. He found a log to sit on and formed the loop or eye with horsehair by twisting a short length of hair between his thumb and forefinger in opposite directions. A sigh of relief blew past his lips as the strands kinked on their own into the eye from tension. *I did it.* He pinched the eye with one hand, then rolled the two separate strands the length of his hand on his leg and formed a tight coil. Next, he rolled the strand away from this body, trying to slow down his breaths and relax because he didn't want one strand to twist itself around the other and create a weak cord. To make sure the double strands remained apart, he released the cordage at the end of the stroke, where he held the eye, keeping the two strands pinned to his leg underneath his hand. His eyes grew round as horsehair twisted together as fast as an arrow launched from a bow.

He tugged hard on the strand to see if it would break. It barely gave. His ma told him about some Bible lesson that explained three strands being stronger than two. Of course she was not talking about horsehair, but the lesson proved the same type of strength— unbreakable. "Yeah, this cord is just as strong."

His mind wandered to things that were braided together…like God the Father, Son, and Holy Spirit. Pa talked about a husband and wife braided together with the Lord for a strong marriage. An image appeared in his mind of a pretty girl in Pekam's village who kept staring at him. He shook his head. "Don't have time for them."

He rushed his horsehair rope to the others and sat by the fire. "This is the answer."

Ross pulled the shirt from his face. He strained to see the rope in the shadows of the fire. "What is it?"

"A rope of some sort?" Jed's brows raised.

"A horsehair rope." Delbert held it over the glowing fire for all to admire.

127

"What for?" Ross scratched his face.

Delbert looked at Ross. He gasped at the bloody claw marks. "You need some of Ma's salve. I wish we'd of packed some."

Jed shrugged his shoulders.

"Stop scraping your face. It's bleedin'. Looks like one of the woman's raw hides hanging on its frame back at the village."

"I can't. It burns. It's driving me crazy. The fire's not helpin' either."

Jed reached some willow bark tea out to him. "Here, drink more."

"It don't do no good." Ross waved him off.

"Well, it won't be long now."

Jed gulped the tea. "What won't be long?"

"Food." Delbert let the words sink in. He sat with a satisfied look pinned on his face.

"What kind of food?" Ross asked.

"Fish."

"How you gonna catch fish with a rope made of horsehair?" Ross poked the fire with a stick.

"By making a weir," Delbert said. "A fishing weir."

"A weir? What's a weir?" Ross grumbled.

"A fish trap. A long one, more like a fence, that crosses the entire creek." Delbert fidgeted with impatience.

"Thought you already had fish traps."

Delbert felt irritation crawl under his skin with each word that spilled out of Ross's mouth. He replied, "I do. This is different."

128

"How so?"

Delbert drew in a sharp breath. "Like I stated, the weir will stretch across the creek."

"You're a fool."

"No, I'm not."

Ross lifted his gaze to Delbert. "Yes, you are."

"I'm inventive."

"Sure ya are." Ross covered his face with the damp shirt and moved back. He felt the need to put distance between him and the heat of the fire. "Do ya even know what that means?"

Jed cleared his throat. He looked as though his amusement faded long ago. "Tell us more, Del. Both of you, quit with the mindless banter. It's gettin' us nowhere."

Delbert tossed the cord to Jed. "With this and some cottonwood poles."

Ross flipped the shirt back over his face and snickered.

Delbert continued. "We can tie the poles together." Sprinkles of rain brushed his head and he looked up, blinking against the drops. "We'll make the trap from bank to bank."

Fingers of lightening zigzagged the sky.

"Thank the good Lord for rain," Ross muttered, his tone lathered with sarcasm.

Thunder cracked in the distance.

The sound of stomping hooves caught Delbert's attention. He craned his neck in their direction and searched the shadows for movement.

"You gonna get the horses or leave 'em down there

for the night?" Jed asked.

"I best go get 'em." Delbert scrambled to the horses. He was able to catch one, but the other two played hard to get. "I'll tie you up so your partners'll stick close." He picketed his gelding and dashed back to the fire. He hoped the other two would be convinced his plan would work. *It has to.*

CHAPTER 14

Delbert hunkered under thick boughs of a fir tree. Even though he bundled in blankets, it was tough to keep dry as the wind whipped the rain straight toward him at a sideways angle. He saw the other two shivering out of the corner of his eyes.

"I'm sure our tents are soaked through," Jed said.

"But at least our blankets'll be warmed by the fire," Ross said.

"So, tell us more about your weir plan, Delbert." Jed tossed a soggy pinecone in the fire and watched it sizzle and spew smoke.

Delbert grabbed two sticks and scooped the pinecone out. He tossed it into the darkness.

"I'll tell you, but first another of Pekam's stories. This may bring us some luck."

"I thought you didn't believe in luck"—Ross grunted—"how long is the story, anyhow?" He yawned.

"I don't, but if you haven't noticed, we're not doin' so good. Anything's bound to improve the odds," Delbert replied. He smiled as he set the sticks by his feet. "This legend's longer, but worth it. Just listen. It may help us. It

131

won't hurt."

Ross scratched his cheeks and neck. He poured water out of his tin cup on the shirt and covered his face. "I'll try and stay awake."

Jed leaned back against a log Delbert drug over for him and propped his purple, swollen ankle on a couple stacked horse blankets. "Okay, tell your story. At least it'll kill some time. And distract from hunger pangs."

Delbert took a swig from his cup and swished it around before swallowing.

Ross heaved a dramatic sigh.

Delbert didn't rush into the tale. He wanted to start the story right. A moment passed before he began. "Pekam's people, the *Sinyekst* or Bull trout people, were dying from starvation—"

Ross ripped the shirt off his face. "They what? You're starting a story with starvation and death in the same sentence? How effective. How is this gonna help us feel better? You think we're gonna die? Is that it? Does Pekam even know where we are? Does anyone?"

Delbert put up his hands. "This has a happy ending. Why do ya think I'm telling it? Settle down and listen for once before assumin' the worst." His red face seared with anger against the rude interruption.

Ross sank back against the log and covered his face. "If I wasn't so tired and weak from *starvation* I'd punch you in the gut." The shirt flung back and forth as Ross tossed his head.

"What did ya say?" Jed sat wide-eyed. "Why don't you two go on and fight it out? Clear the air."

Ross shook his head. "Don't wanna exert my energy on a scrawny rat like him."

Delbert leaped at Ross, knocking him on the ground. He punched his face over and over until Ross was able to grab his arm and flip him over.

Ross pinned him down. "I said I don't wanna exert any energy on a twig like you."

Delbert squirmed under Ross's weight.

Jed scrambled to his feet, grabbed his crutch, and wacked Ross over the head.

"Ha! I saw that coming. You deserve that one you sidewinder," Delbert said to Ross.

Ross fell over, grunted in pain.

Jed said, "Sit down and finish your blasted story. I'm sick of watching you two squabble over mindless stuff. Now sit down!"

Delbert and Ross stood, helped Jed back to his blanket, and took their respective spots by the fire.

Delbert snorted, kicked dirt at Ross.

"Just git on with it. For crying out loud," Jed said. "I'll beat the living daylights out of the likes of you two if this happens again. Now git on with it."

Delbert closed his eyes and shouted above the downpour. "As I said before…the people were dying from starvation. The great evil spirits of the warm land south of here built a mighty dam that spanned the width of the Columbia River and closed off the trail salmon swam for years. The people began to dance and pray day and night. They asked the Creator how to open the salmon trail so the fish, which was their main source of food, could return and reproduce in the mountain streams. My pa says salmon spawn up Hall Creek, but don't make it as far as we are."

133

Jed jerked his head up. "They do?"

"That's what my pa says."

"I'd love to see one. Can you imagine us snaggin' one of those? My uncle told me some of those fish are as big as the little ones in the village." Jed's voice rose to a higher pitch.

"We forgot our hooks, remember?" Ross chimed in.

Jed rolled his eyes.

Images of holding a giant, slimy salmon ran through Delbert's mind. He breathed deep and swore he smelled it cooking over a fire. His gaze shifted to the flames in the pit: blue, orange, red. They danced like a warrior at a Sinyekst celebration, taunting his hunger.

Delbert picked up one of the sticks and poked at the fire as if a fish dangled on its tip and continued. "Coyote heard and came to the rescue." He wanted to move the story along before Ross's snide remarks destroyed Jed's excitement, and his own. "He volunteered to go to the warm country and break up this dam of evil monsters. The people cheered as they envisioned the water spilling over. Coyote set off on his long journey south and after many sundowns, he drew near the dam close to the ocean, or what they called big waters of the Columbia River.

"Coyote shape-shifted into a cooking basket and wiggled himself onto the river. He floated downstream and swirled with the current. There were two sisters, Snipe and Little Snipe, who kept watch over the dam for the evil spirits. They thrived off killing salmon as the fish came close to the stick wall.

"Little Snipe spied the small basket and she squealed with delight. She plucked it out of the river. When she

134

and her sister returned to their tipi, she used the basket as her eating dish. She filled it with salmon and gobbled up the fish. Her sister pounced on Little Snipe. She scolded her for being greedy. Little Snipe quit eating, yet her belly growled with hunger. She set the basket aside. She eyed salmon hanging out the sides of the basket. Her mouth watered. Reaching for the basket, she gasped as it stood empty. Coyote ate the salmon."

The rain let up to a light sprinkle. Delbert gave Ross a sideways glance and grinned—he was still awake with this head tilted back.

At least he isn't snoring.

Jed stirred the coals and banked the fire with a few logs. "What did the Snipe sisters look like?"

"I don't know. I asked Pekam awhile back. He didn't answer." Delbert stared at the fire.

"Maybe the elders want each person to figure that out on their own. See what they wanna see." Ross's big nose poked out of the shirt over his face.

Delbert's gaze jerked to Ross. "You surprise me, Ross. You actually came up with an intelligent answer. I bet you're right."

"Of course I'm right," Ross said. He shook his hands in a sarcastic manner.

Charlie snorted and pawed.

"The other two horses must be close," Jed said.

Delbert scanned the area. All he could hear was the faint hoof-falls of the lone gelding resounding. He waited a bit longer and tried not to let the raised hair on his neck get to him. *Ghosts? Nah.* Nothing. So he continued the story.

135

"As twilight passed, the sisters grew suspicious of the cooking basket that had drifted into their lives. The older sister hurled it into the fire as distrust washed over her like a rushing current. As the basket ricocheted off the finger-like flames, it shape-shifted into a screeching baby boy.

"Little Snipe jumped back in horror. She trembled at the sight, but soon the fright turned to compassion. Peering up at her sister, she begged the girl to allow them to keep the baby and make him their little brother. Snipe refused. Little Snipe begged her sister for hours until Snipe gave in. She ran for the baby and scooped him into her arms and held him to her chest."

"How old are these Snipes s'posed to be?" Ross asked.

"Pekam never shared any details. The elders told the stories. The kids listened. They never question their elders. It's just their way."

"What I don't git is why would they wanna baby to lug around?" Jed asked. "All they do is scream and cry and soil their diapers."

Delbert shrugged. "I figure it's just part of the legend. He gits bigger and smarter; there's a purpose. Movin' along, Little Snipe loved to play with him and in time, Big Snipe did also. But being the rambunctious lad he was, they tied him to a tipi pole before venturing off for the day on their salmon stealing quest as they were afraid he'd fall into the river.

"One morning, coyote realized the dam was almost finished. Hackles rose on the back of his neck. Once the sisters were out of sight and on their way to the Columbia River, he set a wooden spoon on his head and trekked to the dam to finish his task. When his sisters returned, the string was there but nothing was attached to the end. Little Brother was gone.

"Little Snipe began to bawl. The Snipes searched the area. They came across coyote tracks. The girls looked at each other and mirrored round eyes and frowns. To their surprise, they followed tracks leading to the dam. They saw a beast tearing the dam apart. The Snipes collected sticks and began beating coyote over the head. This made Coyote work harder and faster. They could not hurt him nor the wooden spoon.

"In all their excitement, the sisters forgot to call the evil monsters for protection. They forgot about their lost little brother. Before they knew what happened, the dam broke loose. Freed salmon spilled over and swam towards snow-country, up the Columbia River."

Delbert paused. He took a sip of water and fingered the cup. It cooled his sore throat. The rain stopped and the forest grew silent. He couldn't hear Charlie or the other two horses and assumed they were at the gelding's side. "Good ol' herd instincts," he said.

"What are you talking about?" Jed asked.

"The horses. They're quiet."

"Get on with the story. It's late," Jed said, his voice thick with irritation.

Delbert said nothing.

The night as dark as the back of a deep cave, thick clouds shadowed the sky and dampened Delbert's mood. "I wish I could see the stars. Reckon this legend'll have to do," Delbert said.

"Is that it?" Ross asked.

"Thought you were tired or bored. I was wishing you

were asleep." Delbert stood to stretch.

"I hope there's more. Do the fish make it to Pekam's people? What happens to Coyote?" Jed asked.

"I can tell you the rest in the morning. I'm tired and my throat hurts."

Ross dragged the shirt off his face and hurled it at Delbert. "Why would you *wait* 'til morning?"

"Because I'm beat." Delbert yawned.

Jed's lips pressed tight. He tilted his head and scowled.

"I didn't realize you two were likin' the story so well."

Jed leaned in, begged for more. "You said it would bring us a taste of hope."

"All right. I'll finish it tonight."

Ross slid the damp shirt back across his face.

Delbert sat back down on his log and took a big gulp of water. He cleared his throat.

"Here, try some of this," Jed said, holding out his willow juice.

Delbert lowered his chin. He recalled where he'd left off. "Coyote made himself a staff and headed out. He traipsed back to his people with armloads of salmon. He'd traveled for many sundowns before making his way to the Columbia River where he stopped and left part of the salmon. He tramped up the Okanogan River with the rest of the salmon or as Pekam's people say, *in-tee-tee-huh*.

"They all traveled upriver for a few days until he came to another branch of the Okanogan River and again halted. Here he divided the salmon, leaving some and taking the others up the Smilkameen River—"

"That's a lotta dividin' up. Musta been some load of

fish," Jed said.

"Not sure, but Pekam said in the old days, the fish were so thick at times you could almost cross the river walking on their backs." Delbert's mind whirled at the amount of fish they used to have…and how few they'd caught on this trip. "Of course we aren't catching salmon, but the other kinds of fish should be just as abundant."

Ross said, "Yeah, it should be."

Delbert nodded. "They were now in the *Smilkameen* or White Swan territory. Coyote felt pretty lonely. He asked the people for a wife, but the women who he asked laughed at him. The look on his face was filled with sadness and embarrassment. The women told him that they didn't eat salmon, just the back of the necks of mountain goats.

"Insult and surprise washed over Coyote as if someone had spit on his face. He answered them this way, 'You Smilkameen people! In the future you will go far to get the rotted salmon, as you call it.' Coyote turned back from the White Swan territory and left it as it was: jagged and rocky along the river. No trail could be made available for the people where he'd traveled. Their insult would not go unpunished. He led the salmon back to the Okanogan and built falls in the Smilkameen River so no salmon could pass."

"Did he ever get a wife?" Jed asked.

Delbert now understood why the elders taught the stories to their people in the long winter months. He glanced at Ross. The shirt rose and fell to the rhythm of his breath. Unsure if he was awake or not, he answered, "You'll see."

Jed wiggled deep under his blanket.

"Coyote forged up the Okanogan in search of a wife. He found a tribe of people and asked them for one. The people were hungry after seeing the salmon and agreed to let him take an older maid. Coyote was so happy, he let the salmon spawn and hatch in the rivers that link the lakes of the Okanogan. Pekam said salmon breed in that lake to this day."

Delbert cleared his throat and sipped the bark juice.

Ross spoke up. "Is that it? Don't the salmon ever come this way? What's the point of your story if the salmon are over in the Okanogan?"

Delbert could feel heat rise in his face. "I'm not done yet."

"Don't ruin it." Jed glared at Ross. He turned to Delbert and asked, "Where's the Okanogan anyway?"

"Maybe we should quit." Delbert stood and yawned. He intended to turn in for the night.

Jed made a feeble attempt to rise. "Ross, you sidewinder." He turned to Delbert. "We haveta finish the story tonight. I need to know what happens, what's gonna happen to us."

Delbert put out his hand. "Sit down, Jed. I'll finish."

Jed sat back, fists balled up. Delbert could see Jed was about to jump out of his skin.

"Well?" Ross flung his arms out. The shirt managed to remain on his face.

Delbert sat back down and collected his thoughts. "The Okanogan is west of here 'bout three days ride or so. The river runs north and south"—he rubbed a hand down his throat—"Coyote grew tired of his Osoyoos wife. He also grew tired of draggin' salmon up the Okanogan River." Delbert yawned as he stretched and sipped some more bark juice. The heat of the fire relaxed him, but also made him sleepy. He forced himself to keep his eyes open and finish the legend.

"But he kept going. For now. Coyote reached the Penticton people"—Delbert eyed Jed and Ross before confirming—"that's in Canada."

"No foolin'." Ross tore his shirt from his face and threw it at Delbert.

Delbert jumped up, his fist angled for action.

"Enough! You two've already wrecked the story. Finish it once and for all," Jed yelled.

Delbert threw the shirt in the mud. "Like I was saying…" He glared at Ross with a smug look on his face.

"When he reached the Penticton people, in Canada, he asked for a wife. The people didn't give him one right away, but did promise him one later. He agreed and left a large salmon and coursed up river to Vernon, also in Canada."

Delbert looked at the two boys. He waited for a remark. They eyed each other, smiled, and remained silent.

"Coyote asked for a wife with the people in Vernon, but they also just laughed at 'im. This angered Coyote so he said to 'em, 'You will go far and sore-footed before you get your salmon.' They laughed harder. Coyote turned back down river, bringing his salmon with him.

"When he reached the Penticton people, his promised wife was on the arm of another. Coyote huffed off and left behind salmon which had strayed. He made his way south and rested at Dog Lake. There he made the Okanogan Falls and left the rest of his part of the salmon there to spawn for his Okanogan wife.

"Coyote decided to venture back to the Columbia River where the largest of his salmon were kept. This is why no salmon reach the Smilkameen and Vernon People. And why the Pentictons have a handful of salmon that spawn in their territory."

Delbert yawned again, rubbing his temple with calloused fingers. He stared at the fire for a few seconds. The flames almost hypnotized him before continuing on. "Coyote now traveled up the Columbia River. He led his herd of child-sized salmon toward snow-country." Delbert stretched his arms as wide as they would go to try to stir his energy, and for effect.

"He moseyed toward the Sanpoil River until he came to an encampment of people. He asked these people for a wife. To his surprise they gave him a young maiden. Coyote brimmed with excitement. He stopped salmon from traveling upriver and had them spawn and hatch close to the encampment. Today, and Pekam will agree, the Sanpoil peoples' bellies are full of fish meat.

"It wasn't long before Coyote grew tired of his new wife so he left part of the fish with her and continued north. He came to the Arrow Lakes or Sinyekst people, Pekam's people, and asked them for a wife. They laughed and told him that they did not care for salmon. Our food is porcupine, which the great mountains provide for us—"

"What? No. That can't be right. They've got plenty of salmon. They fish twice a year. You've seen what they catch." Ross's flinging hands questioned this part of the legend.

Delbert's leg jigged up and down. He wondered how he could end this. And fast. "Just listen. It's almost over."

142

Ross held up his hands, a mix of disbelief and impatience splashed on his face.

Delbert sat on his hands to make sure he wouldn't punch Ross. "Coyote was angry. He told them their people would tip many canoes over trying to catch the salmon. So Coyote made the trails mountainous, rough, and rocky. He left canoes to travel down the vicious rapids. Coyote snaked through the river bend and traveled to what Pekam calls the People of the Sun or the *Spukanees*. For some reason, he never stopped there, instead he continued on to the *Kalispeliwho* people and asked them for a…"

Ross and Jed said "wife" in unison. They looked at each other and burst out laughing.

Delbert lifted his chin, surprised at their sense of humor. "Yes, a wife. The *Kalispeliwho* people laughed, claiming their prized food was camas. By now Coyote was furious. He was tired of being laughed at. Tired of the wives he'd had or never got. Tired of traveling and herding oversized fish. His mood was as sour as rotten milk. He told them they'd haveta travel far for camas, wearing plenty of holes in their moccasins to trade camas for salmon. Coyote turned back and made the falls tower so the fish could not pass up to these Camas People.

"Coyote headed back for the Columbia River and soon came to the Kettle River. He went up this river to scope out a new wife. When he reached what is now called Canyon Gulch, west of the Kettle River, he found a small village. He asked for a wife. Once again he was laughed at. They told him they did not eat the rotted salmon which was ready to die from making eggs, but that they ate the white fish of the river.

"Coyote agreed that they could keep their white fish.

143

He gave them many bones and named them Northern pike. He informed them they would also have to journey far for salmon. He turned back and headed downriver with his herd of salmon. He built high falls on the Cascade Mountains way up north, in Canadian territory, and no salmon has ever passed over these falls.

"When Coyote again reached the Columbia River, he made huge waterfalls and named them 'Kettle Falls.' Sinyekst people came to greet him, offering him food and shelter. Even though the falls were made for his salmon, Coyote thought he'd share with these Sinyekst people who treated him with love and kindness, but only after the people agreed to give him a wife. Large encampments sprang up at Kettle Falls and Coyote told them many people would come to trade salmon from all directions.

"Coyote settled in with his wife and forgot about leading the salmon. As time went by, he went in search of his own adventures. He left the salmon behind at Kettle Falls so they could come back each year from the Big Waters of the ocean and spawn. Since Coyote broke the mighty dam the evil spirits kept charge of, the salmon returned and flourished. This was back in the days of the Animal People. Pekam's people."

Delbert sat in silence for a while. So did the other two. He hoped they would soak in a bit of hope from the story. Images of salmon came to mind and he pondered them for a bit. Finally, he skipped into the calm like a flat rock against water, speaking with passion. "It may not be salmon in our creek, but there are trout. Trout with red bellies and we can catch 'em. We will catch 'em!"

"Yeah, and we don't need no wife to get the job done neither." Jed crossed his arms.

Ross added, "That's for sure. What do you have in

mind, Del?"

"We need to build this weir."

Jed pointed to his ankle.

"I know. You can sit and twist the tail hair into the cording I need ... by this nice cozy fire." Delbert gave him a broad smile.

"Is there enough tail hair with just your gelding?" Ross asked.

Delbert thought about the lone horse. "I think so. But I'm sure in the morning the others will be there. I've already cut off a nice chunk." He held up a fistful of hair to the light of the fire.

Chapter 15

July 21, 1867
Day Seven

Delbert woke to the sound of rain beating on his dirt-stained canvas tent. Darkness from clouds in the sky blocked the morning glow. He shivered under the blankets. He thought about getting up and starting a fire. But couldn't seem to move. Laying around wouldn't get his blood pumping. "I should get up and move." He groaned and rolled over.

But his body felt stiff, and so did his throat. It was all he could do to lift his eyelids. He rolled over to the other side and propped himself on his elbows, willing himself to rise and check the fire. He couldn't see anything in the pitch black. Not even his hand inches from his runny nose. He sniffed and groaned.

He reached out. His fingers groped the ground. They felt cold, wet dirt. Mud.

"Great. I have a stream running through my tent." His hands roamed the soggy ground until his fingers felt the cold leather of his boots. He tossed his blanket aside

147

and pulled them on. The insides were dry and for that he was thankful.

The cry of a mountain lion sliced through pounding rain. The hairs on his neck stood straight up and a chill ran down his back. He heard Charlie snort and whinny. Delbert waited for the answer of the other horses. None came. His gelding pawed the ground and cried out to the other horses.

The mountain lion thrust a deep, guttural growl from his mouth. Delbert jumped to his feet and hit his head on the tent. He dropped to his knees and crawled outside. The fire burnt out long ago. He held his breath. Crickets made it hard to listen for the direction of the mountain lion. He sensed the cat's glowing eyes on him. His stomach twisted in fear. He tried to breathe normal in spite of his trembling body. His heart beat so fast he thought it would burst right out of his chest. He almost wished it would so he could find relief.

Delbert shuffled to the fire pit. He heard another bloodcurdling scream from the beast, the snap of a tree branch, and the sound of hooves thundering away.

"What should I do? Call for help? Jed can't stand. Ross's eyes and face are still swollen. Should I make the fire? Is there dry tinder? Or do I go back to bed? Lord, need a little help here…"

He looked up.

Delbert resigned to the fact he could do nothing. He turned around as he heard the horses run off. "Jed. Ross." No answer. "Great. How will we get back to the village?" He stood motionless in the dark and listened for the slightest sign of life. He tilted his head, nose up, and closed his eyes as if that would help. Sniffed the air. He sighed. "The lion must have chased after the plump horses rather than hang back for the likes of me—not much on these here bones." He patted his ribs and noticed his pants hung half way down his hips. After cinching his belt tight.

Not knowing what to do, he shuffled back to his tent, body still trembling. He fumbled around and found dry moss and pine needles. While he took baby steps and held his hands out to block a possible fall, he made his way back to the circle of rocks that held wet ashes. The fir braches offered some protection. The smell of burnt wood wafted around him. Even though blackness surrounded him, he found a flat, large rock, laid it in the fire pit, and placed a pinch of tinder on it. He pulled his rock and flint piece out of his pant pocket. A couple of sparks and he could smell a wisp of smoke. He blew in its direction, moving air a tiny bit. Soon a speck of flame emerged.

Delbert added more moss and twigs until enough light gave way to gather bigger sticks and toss them on. The fire now strong enough to sustain for a couple of hours, he quit shivering, and stumbled back to his tent to sleep until daylight.

What if the lion lingered behind? He tossed and turned until his thoughts settled down, and he felt heavy eyelids close.

Daylight broke over the mountains and illuminated a dark, gray horizon. Delbert lay there, eyes closed. *Did a mountain lion come or was it a bad dream?* Muffled sounds floated through his tent. He pulled his blanket over his head, not yet ready to show his face.

"Delbert, you awake yet?" Jed threw stones at his tent.

"I thought you was gonna make some kinda fish-catchin' contraption," Ross said.

Jed snickered. "Yeah, come on. We wanna watch you build this fishin' weir thing."

Delbert snapped his blanket off his face and frowned. "Why're they so blasted jolly?" He said. "Did they not hear the mountain lion? How could they miss all the uproar?" He sat up and pulled on his boots. "I'm comin'." He crawled out of his tent, mood brightening at the sight of a blazing fire. "How'd you get the fire so big with such wet wood?"

Ross gave Jed a sideways glance, flashing him a ruthless grin. "Old Indian trick."

"Yeah. I bet. What's with you two anyway? Did ya not hear the mountain lion almost eat us for supper last night? Or maybe this morning. Either way it was as black as those burnt coals outside." Delbert motioned to a piece of charred wood on the outside of the rock fire pit.

"What lion? Heck, I slept mighty solid." Ross sat on a log with his legs stretched out.

Jed waved a stick around in the air, swatted flies, and held up his bark juice. "I didn't hear a thing. What are ya talkin' about?" He stopped, pointed the stick at Delbert and stated, "Maybe it was coyote, comin' for salmon." The stick bobbed in the air as if spearing fish.

"Or one of his wives." Ross looked around and acted like he was coyote looking for a lost wife.

Delbert watched Ross and Jed mock him. Crossing his arms over his chest, he asked, "Look around. Do you see anything missin'?"

Jed and Ross scanned the mountains, shaking their ragged-looking heads.

"Not up there." Delbert wondered why he asked these two tinhorns to come in the first place. He was sick of Ross's pessimist outlook displayed the previous night, and now his mocking attitude. Even Jed was on edge. This morning, he heard Ross sing a new tune, a joyful one that Delbert wanted to slap off his lips. "Open your eyes. What are we missing?" Delbert asked. He tried to hold his temper in check.

"I don't know, Del. Why don't ya fill us in?" Ross crossed his arms and give Delbert a defiant look.

"Ah, the ugly's back. That's what we're used to. An attitude that drips with the sweet smell of vinegar. You need to close your trap before I ring your neck."

Jed threw sticks at both of them. "Enough! Del, just tell us."

Delbert stared at the fire and with enormous control stated, "All the horses have now run off. We're outta food. We're weak, cranky, and now have to *walk* back to the village. You two no-account critters are of no use—"

"Hold on now. That's not right. I didn't get hurt on purpose and Ross didn't chase the wasps down and force them to sting his face." Jed tried to jump to his feet.

Delbert held his hands out. "I'm sorry, Jed. Sit down. I'm outta line. It's not your fault. It's no one's fault. We… I'm tired and hungry."

Ross rubbed his hot, itchy, swollen face. "You were right the first time. We're all tired and starved half to death. How are we gonna get back? Do you think the horses are all right? Did the cougar kill them?"

"I hope they aren't dead," Jed said. "How will we get back? I can't walk out. What are we gonna do? Do you think the horses are alive?"

151

Delbert held his hands up. "I don't think the horses are dead. They're probably close by. Horses run off and tend to circle back. You two know that." He paused. "So, here's my plan." Delbert drew lines in the dirt with a stick. "I have to gather cottonwood poles. Lots of 'em." He drew fish swimming up to the lines, set like a fence, in the dirt. "The horsehair is here somewhere,"—Jed searched the ground—"Oh, yeah, it's in my saddlebag. You two can make rope out of horsehair and if needed, I can cut and peel willow bark and use those fibers, too."

"I think we can manage that," Ross said, excitement rung in his voice. "Wait. I don't know how to make rope out of anything. Do you, Jed?" His face shown confusion mixed with exasperation.

Jed shook his head. "Never have done that."

"It's what I showed you earlier, but a whole lot longer. Pekam taught me. I've practiced and can remember how to add the length we need. It's simple. It just takes time."

Jed nodded. "I suppose so."

"Well, let's get to work." Delbert hummed as he fetched the horsehair. Heaviness floated off his shoulders. His steps eased.

CHAPTER 16

The boys hunkered around the fire while rain drizzled around them in dawn's pink glow. Tree branches managed to keep them somewhat dry. As long as the fire burned bright, they stayed warm. His britches hung loose. He glanced at the other two. Theirs sagged on their hips as well. Ross cinched up his belt a few notches, and the end of the leather stuck out to the side. Jed raised his hands to the fire, his ankle propped up on a wet, mud-encrusted horse blanket.

"Should we go ahead and get started?" asked Delbert.

"We got nothin' better to do," Ross answered. "The faster this weir goes up, the quicker we got vittles."

Delbert divided the horsehair into two hunks and handed Ross and Jed each their share. He held a pine needle-sized chunk back to demonstrate the cording method. But first took a few minutes to fiddle with the hair. He needed to figure out how to show Jed and Ross the right way.

"You ready yet?" Ross's stomach orchestrated a growling harmony.

"I need to get this right. Only done it a few times…"

"Get what right?" Ross asked.

"How to start it. See, you have to roll the hair in opposite directions and flip it around to make this starting loop. It's called an eye. Once I get this…"

Jed and Ross leaned in close.

"There. This is the loop that begins the cording." Delbert held up his work.

Jed and Ross separated a few strands of the tail hair and rolled it like Delbert. They made their loops the size of a silver dollar.

Jed held his up. "How come mine's so big?"

Delbert chuckled. "Because you made it that way. It's too loose. But don't worry, you'll get it." He showed Jed again how he formed the starting eye small and tight.

Ross watched closely.

Each made their loop smaller this time.

"That's good, but it needs to be even tighter. You both practice. I'm going to rustle up some berries and roots. By the time I return, your loops should be the size we need.

"Okay. I could use a little something in my belly," Jed admitted.

"Me, too. I can't concentrate with my stomach complaining like it is," Ross said.

"Here, drink this. It'll help fill the gap." Delbert filled each boy's cup with water and set it beside them. "I'll be back soon. I think I'll check out the horse tracks. See what direction they may've taken. Hopefully they're close by."

A couple hours later, Delbert returned with a cup full of service berries and a pouch full of roots: wild carrots and potatoes.

"I already ate mine, so you boys can split this up. There's not much out there yet. Too early in the season. That or we are too low." Delbert slid to the damp ground. A drizzle fell from dark clouds.

Jed and Ross looked at the meager rations and at each other. They accepted the offering, savoring the berries and roots in their parched mouths, a little at a time.

Delbert glanced down at three heavy rocks holding Ross's work in place. He clasped the hair, lifted the rock, and held the loop up for inspection. "This is fine. Real fine."

"Really?"

"Uh-huh. Nice and tight. Like Pekam showed me." He put the loop back under the rock.

Jed shoved the last of the roots in his mouth, savoring the flavor. He picked up one of his loops. "How about this one?"

Delbert fingered the cord. "Yep, mighty fine work, Jed. I think you guys are ready to move on." Delbert picked up his looped strand and held it out. "There are two ways to roll the cords: with your fingers or on your leg. We can start with our fingers, but will need to switch to rolling the hair on our legs once the cord gets longer because it'll be faster."

Delbert rolled the two ends of the horsehair about an inch and rested the hair cording on his leg. "The hair has to be rolled away from you. Like this." Delbert demonstrated. "The two strands haveta stay separate or it won't work. When we let go, which I'll show ya in a minute, the ends will twist by themselves."

Delbert showed Ross and Jed how to roll the fibers so they twisted tight, forming the thin rope they needed to secure the poles for the weir.

Ross tilted his head up and down so his blurred vision could focus on his efforts. He and Jed worked in silence as Delbert looked on. Rain bounced off tree branches and made the fire dance. Wet fingers and horsehair made for hard work.

As one end of the cord came near, Delbert rolled added hair into it before running out. "When the end of the cord is close, we need to add more tail hair in order to keep the same thickness or the two strands of the cord'll be uneven and one strand'll wind around the other, not twist, and the cord will lose strength."

"Why didn't you use the mane for this?" Jed asked.

"It's softer, which we don't need. What we do need is the length of the tail for the weir. Remember, this is gonna stretch across the creek."

Jed stroked his cord. "Feels pretty soft to me. But I get how we need the length." He looked toward to creek.

When the boys got the hang of making the rope, Delbert grabbed the hatchet and headed out to gather cottonwood poles.

There was no shortage of young trees to use for weir poles. And he had no idea how many to harvest, so he guessed. He lumbered up the river and chopped down small poles. His supply looked meager. "I can't be as picky as Pekam and his family since we're runnin' short on time."

Once Delbert cut down several young cottonwood trees, he de-limbed them, left the bark on, and chopped off the tops. Small in diameter, the poles stood a foot

CARMEN PEONE

taller than Delbert. Much higher and he wouldn't be able to handle pounding them into the creek bed by himself.

He dragged the poles to the sand and stacked them on the bank. They reminded him of a raft. All he'd need to do was tie them together. He worked for several more hours and after he had a couple dozen laid out, thanked the Lord for making the creek slim.

Ross and Jed watched Delbert drag in the poles.

"Think we'll have enough rope?" Jed asked.

"That's what I've been wondering." Ross fingered the cord. "It'll be close."

Delbert mopped sweat off his brow with his shirtsleeve. "Yeah. We'll have enough. I sure wish I had Charlie to help me drag these poles in." He sat down, chest heaving. His arms felt like they would fall off and his back ached. *Lord, give me strength to finish this.* He scooped up several handfuls of water. A fish jumped in front of him. "Hope this is a sign you'll provide for us." Delbert's spirits lifted as he sat and waited for fish to jump.

His aching back screamed, so he stretched. He felt sleep sucking him down into a black hole. The muscle at the corner of his eyes twitched. Felt heavy. He shuffled to the others. "How's it going up here?" All too thin boys with defeated looks on their faces made Delbert turn this thought on his ma, sewing by a fire in the evenings. He said in a whisper, "Good, but I miss Ma and her cooking. I miss my family." He shook his head. "What I need to do is prove to Pa and Pekam I can survive in the wild. To be a man."

"Delbert, did ya hear me?"

"Yeah. I heard ya."

"Well, do ya think we'll have enough rope? We're runnin' low on tail hair." Ross repeated.

Delbert looked at the rope they had, the hair that was left, and the pile of logs. He watched the current drift down the creek. "I think so. I know I don't have room for error." Delbert twisted to the side and wrung out the front of his shirt. "I wish this rain would let up."

Jed pulled a few strands of horsehair out, set it on the cord, and rolled it on his leg. He rolled away from his body in a slow, long stroke. "Glad it's not a complete downpour."

"It could be worse." Delbert searched the ground for any semblance of food. "Best get back to work. I'll need some rope soon."

Ross held up a long piece. "Will this work?"

"Ya. I'll start with this and see how far I get." Delbert stuffed the rope into his back pocket with its tail trailing behind.

Ross called out, "Don't let the brush pull it out of your pocket. Like you said, there's no room for error."

Delbert nodded and waved.

"Delbert," Jed said. "How ya gonna prop those poles up? I know this isn't a spring current, but still…"

Delbert turned to the stack of poles and groaned. His gaze stuck on the cottonwood, he shoved his hands on his hips. "I need to go back out and cut down some smaller poles to anchor the cottonwoods. They'll form a tipped 'T'." He put his hands together in the shape he meant. Frustration swarmed him like flies on rotted meat and he kicked the ground. He grunted and stumbled off to get the hatchet.

He returned with five young, sturdy lodge pole pine

poles to use for the "T" anchor posts and laid them on the ground. It was a good start. He picked up two cottonwood poles and lined them up on the beach next to one another. He pulled out horsehair rope from his back pocket and tied the cottonwood poles together toward the top. He eyed his work, impressed with its sturdiness, and for the first time in a long time felt a sense of pride.

"This does look mighty fine. Now, I need more rope for the bottom."

Once he'd added a third and fourth pole, he decided to stop. He studied the current and wondered if with waist deep water, the creek would be strong enough to flop someone like him over and carry 'em downriver before they have the chance to yell for help.

He dragged the section of poles closer to the creek and set them down. He pulled off his boots and socks, rolled up his pant legs, and dipped a toe in the creek, inching his way in. "These blasted rocks're gonna cut up my feet."

He heard Ross and Jed snicker as they sat by the fire. "Those skunks better stop laughing or I'll shove 'em in and see how they like it." He kept his gaze to the creek. A shiver ran down Delbert's back as he dipped his body into the frigid water.

Delbert bent down and lifted up one cottonwood pole section. *No room for error.* He dragged the set of poles into the water. The cold made him grit his teeth. His feet and ankles stung. *I can do this.* He winced from sharp rocks on bare feet. "Oh no! I forgot the anchor pole and the hatchet," he grumbled.

He let loose a pent-up bellow that echoed through the mountains. Tension in his gut released and tight

159

muscles relaxed. He drug the waterlogged poles back and knocked off patches of bark. Slick, wet cottonwood stunk so bad his nose hairs felt like they'd singed right off his nostrils. The poles slipped from his aching fingers. Delbert wiped the sharp odor from his nose with a handful of grass. He shoved the hatchet in his back pocket and snatched up one of the anchor poles.

He still refused to look toward the other two boys. Sorry they were sick, he wished they could help—extra hands to make the load light. *But I need to prove myself. To everyone.*

Delbert wrapped his fingers around the slimy middle poles, struggled to keep skin on horsehair for a better grip, and lifted the fence structure upright. He sucked in a deep breath and held it against the woody stench, and leaned the poles against his shoulder. His muscles burned. When he turned to hammer the anchor pole into the creek bed with the blunt end of the hatchet, he lifted his arm to tie on the anchor pole which caused the set of cottonwoods to roll off and drift down the creek.

"No!" He hit the water with his fists. "Why? What next?" he yelled.

He reached out to catch the poles, but they brushed against the tips of his fingers and slipped away. His balance wavered and he plunged into the creek, came up and let out a deep, angry grunt, then heaved the hatchet and anchor pole onto the bank. He dove back in and swam with hard, even strokes.

Stroke after stroke he swam, until his fingers brushed the poles. He took hold of the horsehair rope with his fingers slipping between the poles and dragged the set to shore. Land felt solid as he flopped in the sand. Adrenalin sped through his veins. He tried to catch his breath, but his lungs felt like they were on fire. All he could do was roll onto his side and curl into a ball.

After his breathing slowed and the adrenalin drained from him, he rose to his feet and dragged the set of cottonwood poles back to where he began. *I'm glad this cottonwood's light, even waterlogged.* He stumbled back in an attempt to dodge jagged rocks and sharp fir and pinecones that poked his bare feet.

"Ouch!" He picked off a pinecone stuck to the bottom of his foot. Scrapes and blood etched his soles. But hunger drove him forward.

Delbert peered at gray clouds. He hoped to see where the sun hung, but thick coverage blocked his view. *Midday has to be near.* Feelings of hopelessness blanketed his body. *I'm so tired. Hungry.* The poles now seemed heavy, but he made it back and dropped them to the ground. Weathered hands rested on his knees, he bent over. Energy drained from his body as quick as burned up tinder. His gut felt tight. Empty. *I need food. Sleep.*

He trudged back to the fire in dripping clothes and plunked down on a log. He shook his head and water sprayed in all directions. A familiar sizzle of water on hot rocks soothed his edgy nerves. He'd always loved that sound.

Jed and Ross stared at him, wide-eyed.

"You all right?" Concern spread over Ross's face. He rested a section of unfinished cording on his lap.

"Maybe you need to get dry clothes on," Jed offered.

"Del, did ya hear me?" Ross asked, his voice a notch louder.

Delbert nodded. But he didn't move. Or speak.

Jed laid his cording on the ground and leaned over to

161

wiggle his way to his feet. Ross grabbed hold of his arm. "Sit down. I'll help 'im."

Jed settled back and fidgeted with the rope clutched in his fingers. He peered at Delbert, at Ross, and back at Delbert. "What can I do to help? I don't wanna sit here twiddlin' my thumbs."

"I can't do this," Delbert said. "The current's too strong. It's sucking me in. I'm so tired."

Ross handed his work to Jed. "Jed can finish the ropes. He's got it down. I can't see good enough with these puffy eyes…the hair's so small…or thin to finish the ropes. But I can hold the anchor poles while you tie them to cottonwoods."

Delbert noticed how little Ross accomplished. Nodding, he said, "I'll change first."

Ross watched Delbert stumble to his tent and guzzle more water. His mouth dry and sticky, he couldn't drink enough water to quench his thirst. It wasn't long before his bladder complained so he got up and headed to a bush. When he came back, he helped Jed up to do the same.

Afterward, Ross filled two cups for Jed: one with bark juice and the other with water. "I thought he'd be out by now. Hey, Del, let's get goin'!"

No answer.

"Del, you changed?"

"I hope he's not in there fuming," Jed said.

Ross sauntered to the tent and rapped on it. No

answer. "I'm comin' in." Ross lifted the flap and crawled in. He saw Delbert sound asleep, snoring like a baby. A pile of wet clothes sprawled on the damp dirt floor. Irritation and impatience shimmied up Ross's nerves. "I'll be." He fought his rising anger, but after seeing how rugged Delbert appeared, Ross couldn't help but feel sorry for him. "Reckon you need some shut-eye."

Ross ambled back to the fire and plopped down on a log. "His fire's snuffed out."

"You're kidding me."

"Nope. In there sawin' logs."

"We should've helped him." Ross's gaze fell to the ground.

"No. He needs to prove himself."

"Prove himself? Why?"

"Haven't you been listenin' to what he's been chattering about? Not being as worthy as his pa?" The muscle in Ross's jaw tightened. "His pa's proud of him. Delbert's too bullheaded to see it. His pa doesn't care if Del wants to dig for rocks, as long as he's happy. Ranching isn't for everyone. There's plenty of things he's smart about...this isn't one of 'em."

Jed nodded in agreement. "More 'n likely. I guess I can see his mama's smarts in 'im." He picked up the cording and rolled more horsehair. "Why do ya give 'im such a hard time?"

Ross smiled. "Sharpens the backbone."

Jed shook his head, not letting Ross see the grin on his face.

"What do we do now?" Jed asked.

"You keep twisting that hair and I'll go scavenge

163

some food. We have to eat or we'll end up buzzard bait."

"Okay. Stay away from them wasps." Jed snickered. "Can ya even see enough to get some grub? I hope you don't go mistaken good berries for ones that'll poison us."

"I'll manage," Ross said over his shoulder.

CHAPTER 17

The rain stopped, clouds parted, and the sun radiated rays that glittered light on wet leaves. A double rainbow broke over the hills. Birds chirped and chipmunks played.

Delbert crawled out of his tent. He saw Jed stoking the fire. He hesitated to walk over and join him, but couldn't hide his shame of falling asleep much longer. Delbert sat down on his usual log. He searched the area for sign of horses, but saw none. "This is gonna be a long walk back." He looked up, saw the rainbow. "Hope that's a good sign."

Jed nodded. "How ya feel?"

Delbert nodded. "Better." Glancing around, he asked, "Where's Ross?"

"Went in search of food."

"Where?"

Jed pointed west. "That way."

"Oh great. How long ago?"

"Right after he discovered you snoring."

Delbert's face spread from pink to red. He watched chipmunks play and birds flutter from branch to branch. After watching for a moment, he rubbed the sleep out of his eyes. "Can't believe I fell asleep." He watched Jed roll the horsehair on his leg, twisting the two lengths into a nice strong rope. "You're gettin' good at that."

"Trying to." He kept rolling. "I kinda like it. I feel like I'm contributing something to your weir. And our survival."

Delbert stared at his empty hands. "Wish we had somethin' to eat." He poked the coals around in the fire and spread them out flat. Sparks shot up. He tossed a few more logs on the fire and stopped one from rolling out. He swung it back on top of the coals. "Best keep this goin'. Never know."

"I can smell the fish. See the flames cooking it. Taste the meat. Umm."

Delbert brightened. "Yeah. I'm glad Ross's gone. I'm not up for his sarcasm," he said. "Well, I'm gonna go tie some more poles together. Got some rope for me?"

Jed held up a long strand, his grin so wide dirty teeth peered from behind red, cracked lips. He licked blood off them and wiped his mouth with his shirtsleeve. "I'm not up for it either."

"Fine work." Delbert whisked the rope out of Jed's hand and marched to the bank. While he set out poles, his drenched clothes came to mind. He jogged back to the tent, snatched his clothes from the ground, strung them out by the fire. "I need to save my strength. Especially if Ross isn't back soon. Or is empty-handed. I'll have to go looking for him. Waste more time. I've already wasted enough with a stupid nap."

Jed agreed.

Delbert plodded back to his task.

Delbert pulled his focus back to his work and

166

arranged four poles side by side. He tied them together with Jed's rope and worked until all the poles were tied at the top in sets of four. Then went to get more rope.

When Delbert walked up, Jed was rolling the last of the rope on his leg. "All I need to do is tie the ends together."

Warmth filled the late afternoon air and steam rose from the ground. Delbert mopped sweat from his brow with the shirt Ross used to cool the sting from his face. "No sign of Ross yet, huh?" He took a big gulp of water and pretended it was a cup of fresh milk. "We have to keep drinking this or we don't survive."

"Yeah, I know. Haven't seen 'im."

"Kinda stuck 'til he gets back." Delbert rubbed his face. He pulled up his pants before sitting on a log.

Jed noticed. "I got up to relieve myself this morning and my britches almost hit the dirt. I hadn't even undone 'em yet."

"Seven days with little food. Our bones are showing through like starved calves."

"Let's hope Ross found something."

They heard footsteps, crackling of twigs and rustling of leaves. Ross's head appeared, a scowl on his face.

"What'd ya turn up?" Jed asked.

"Not much more'n chicken scratch, but it's something. Seems the bears are just as starved as we are. Most of the berries are gone. I scavenged a few anyhow, and a couple roots, but that's all." Ross spread his coat on the ground and knelt on it. He tipped his pouch upside-down and a fistful of berries rolled out. He shook the pouch and four wild carrot roots rolled onto the jacket. They were dirty, but a bath with grass and they'd be

167

mighty fine eating. He tossed the pouch to the side and said matter-of-factly, "This is it."

Delbert leaned forward. "I reckon it's better'n nothin'."

Ross scooped up a couple of berries and roots and handed them to Jed.

Jed popped them in his mouth. The flavor burst with one bite and a blend of sweet and tart poured out. Ross and Delbert did the same. Didn't take long before it was all gone. An awkward silence fell between them.

Delbert fingered some rocks.

Ross tossed on another log.

Jed fiddled with his rope.

After a moment, Delbert looked at Ross. "I did get the poles sorted and tied. Need more rope. I have to tie the bottom ends of all the sets of four. After that we can put 'em up and pound 'em in." Delbert studied Ross's face. The swelling came down, but his face was still red-hot and scratch marks made his face resemble cottonwood bark. Swollen cottonwood bark. "Ready?"

Ross scratched his face. "Better get goin'."

Jed held out the rest of the rope. Ross ran his fingers over the cording. "You make this?"

"Yep."

"Sure is dandy work."

Jed beamed. "Delbert thought so, too."

"His pa'd be proud." Delbert added.

Jed's face fell. Delbert recognized the look. *I'll bet he's homesick. His ma's home-cooked meals. His pa's teasing. He wants his life back. We all do.*

Delbert swallowed tightness from his throat, got up,

and rushed to the bank. Ross followed. Delbert set to tying poles together and instructed Ross on how to set the anchor poles at an angle to be tied to the weir poles.

Jed limped his way toward them.

"What're you doin'?" Ross hurried to his side.

"I'm tired of being stuck up there. Besides, my ankle could use a good soakin'. Ease the achin'."

Ross looked around. "You're swayin' like a willow in the breeze. Where's your bark juice?"

"I ran out a long time ago. Besides, I don't need it anymore, just a good soakin'." Ross struggled to help Jed to the water. Jed's tall frame hovered over him, but he was able to slink to the ground and slid his ankle into the creek. The cool liquid swirled around his legs.

"Whoa, that stings." He grit his teeth until a numbing sensation set in. His shoulders relaxed and his body slumped. He focused as well as he could while Delbert instructed the next step.

Delbert lifted the segment of cottonwood poles and dragged them into the water. Ross followed behind with an anchoring pole, hatchet, and rope. Delbert stood the segment of poles upright while Ross took the hatchet and pounded the lodge pole into the creek bed at an angle facing the middle of the pole section Delbert held. Delbert leaned the section of poles against the lodge pole and tied them together. They repeated this until the fence weir reached the other side of the creek.

"Glad this is narrow," Ross exclaimed.

Delbert tied off the last of the cottonwood segment to the final anchor pole. "We're almost done."

They slogged back across the creek. Delbert shifted his weight from one leg to the other.

Ross watched him. "What?"

"One more thing." He cleared his throat. "We need to secure the weir with stones. We run them along the base…on both sides." He cleared his throat again. "Hope I'm not gettin' sick."

"You're kidding, right?"

"Nope. Not about that."

Ross searched the ground. "Glad we're in rocky territory."

Delbert and Ross set stones along the base of the weir and finished as evening shadows set in.

"Better get moving," Delbert said. He and Ross helped Jed hobble to the fire. Delbert handed them more water to keep hydrated. He drank a cupful himself. Delbert felt too weary for stories tonight. He stared at the fire. Animals made noises in the forest. An owl's hoot echoed through the trees. Delbert held his hands out in front of the fire. A drop of rain fell on Delbert's nose. He wiped it away and realized he'd not thought about the weather all afternoon. *Please, Lord, not another downpour.*

Lightening streaked the sky and glowed through clouds. Seconds later, thunder cracked against the mountains. A few more raindrops made the flames flicker. Delbert watched Ross help Jed to his tent before heading to his own. Delbert felt bad as he watched Jed scoot inside, but his arms felt like lead. He banked the fire before wobbling to bed.

CHAPTER 18

July 22, 1867
Day Eight

The steady *tap, tap, tap* of raindrops landing on the canvas stirred Delbert awake. Light squeezed through the tent. Delbert blinked. He strained to open his eyes. They felt plastered shut. Muscles stiff, stomach tight, he groaned. "I'm sick. I need more sleep." He rolled over, covered his head, and willed his mind to shut down. But thoughts of the weir picked at him like a woodpecker to a tree.

Get up. Check the weir. Get up. Now! "No," he said.

"Is that you, Del?" Jed said. "You awake yet?"

"I'm awake."

"Get up. Daylight's burnin'. Come on, let's check for fish. Ross's in the bushes. We didn't wanna go down there without you." Jed's voice bounced off the tent walls.

"Hold your horses." Delbert threw his blanket aside. He heard the sound of rain outside and moaned. He straggled out of the tent. Rain pelted his face.

Ross strode up. "It's about time you wake up. Day's half gone."

Delbert sneered.

Ross and Delbert took hold of Jed, ready to head to the creek.

"Hey! Watch out," Jed hollered.

"We're not trying to dump you," Ross said.

"Just git me to the water and set me down."

Delbert hit the make-shift crutch. "Quit bumping us and we can."

They plopped Jed on the ground. Delbert leaned as close as he could and peered in. Armfuls of red bellied trout milled around and nudged the weir, swam more circles, and prodded the fence line again as the current edged them closer. Water rippled as fish swirled, jumped and bumped the weir. It looked as though they were trying to break down the cottonwood wall. But it held tight.

"We did it!" Ross broke into one of his chicken-like dances.

Delbert rushed in, dipped hands, and darted from trout to trout. Ross stopped dancing and followed suit. Delbert reached for fish, but the wiggly, slimy creatures slipped through his grip each time. He whooped and hollered.

"I got one," Ross shouted. But as quick as his words came, the fish slithered back into the water.

Delbert plunged his hands in and tracked a fish, but it whizzed away. He swiped rain drops from his eyes.

Jed scooted into the water, chest high, as fish darted around him. He grabbed, missed, shouted, and toppled over. He shoved himself back to a sitting position. "Git back here!" He spanked the water.

172

Delbert stated the obvious. "We didn't think through how we'd catch the fish once they were at the weir."

"How does Pekam do it?" Jed asked.

"They use nets and spears."

"Out of?"

"Sticks and twine."

"Made out of?"

"Don't rightly know. Never watched 'em make one. I reckon hemp or tule fibers."

Ross stopped turning in circles and let the fish escape. "We could have used the horsehair."

Jed laughed. "Yeah, if they hadn't run off."

"We could use the fibers from willow bark, or off Indian Hemp." Delbert's focus stuck on a huge black fish with a red band running down the length of its belly. It swam the length of the weir. Drizzle turned into a downpour that pelted the creek and made it hard to see the swarming trout.

Jed sat in icy water and shivered. He sputtered, "I'll go back and sit by the fire while you two figure that one out. When you find fibers, give 'em to me. I'll twist you up some rope."

They all laughed and carried on and splashed each other. Not one of them thought about scaring fish away.

"We need to get Jed up to the fire before he freezes." Ross sloshed to Jed's side, Delbert on the other. They lifted him up and dragged him back to camp.

Delbert scrounged around and found dry clothes for Jed. He checked on the clothes he'd spread out earlier. Since he forgot to pick them up the previous night, rain soaked them. He and Ross found other dry clothes—their

173

last pair. Jed changed with the help of his friends and they moved by the fire to warm up and devise a plan. Fortunately, the rain let up. Dark clouds passed and only a light mist fell.

Delbert began. "We can either squander time to gather fibers from bark and bushes, or go back to building fish traps."

"I say fish traps." Jed blinked away drops landing on his eyelashes that fell from fir branches. He wrapped a blanket around his shoulders and placed his cup of water close to the fire.

"That'd be quicker," Ross agreed.

"Okay, let's go hunt some worms. I don't feel like chasing after crickets." Delbert turned to Jed. "Will you get some sticks ready? Slice the ends? Here's my knife."

Jed nodded.

"I'll dig for worms," Ross offered. He picked up a stick and stirred hot coals. "And bank this fire. We can't let it go out."

"I'll make the traps." Delbert clapped his hands to spur them on. He gathered sticks for Jed and rambled to the creek. He studied the creek to determine the best spot for the traps—deep pools, slow current. He collected more sticks and inserted them into the creek bed from the bank out into deeper water in order to form the heart-shaped trap. His excitement mounted with each stick. He completed five traps before checking on Jed and Ross.

Delbert found Ross and his dirt-stained fingers pushing worms into slits of the sticks, twelve in all. When done, Ross and Delbert helped Jed back by the creek. He held a crutch stick in one hand and clutched Ross's

174

shoulder with the other. Delbert held on to the back of Jed's shirt.

"Slow down, Jed. You're pullin' me over." Ross braced himself.

"Sorry." Jed brightened with excitement. Dirty, yellow teeth shone through his grin.

At the water's edge, Delbert and Ross righted themselves before tipping over. Jed grabbed their shirts and pulled hard.

"I told you to slow down," Ross said.

Jed hit Ross with his crutch. "I can't help it."

Delbert gripped the back of Ross's shirt just to make sure they were stable. Then pulled off his boots and socks. He looked at Jed and smiled. His gaze shifted to Ross. "Hand me a stick." He extended his hand.

Ross slapped a stick into his open palm.

Delbert inserted the stick into the first trap, worm down. Ross handed Delbert sticks with bait for all the rest as he waded around and across the creek. "I should've put my wet clothes back on."

"Yeah, why did we change into dry clothes?" Ross asked.

"Because you two are smart." Jed smiled.

Delbert splashed water on Jed.

"Stop! I'm finally dry and warm."

Ross grinned. "Let's get him."

Delbert laughed. "Let's get these fish."

He thrust a single baited stick into the sand inside three heart-shaped traps. He smiled at the others.

They waved as Delbert pushed toward them, against

the current.

"We can either wait here, or go back to the fire and dry off," Delbert stated.

"Back by the fire. Maybe you could tell us another story to kill the time." Jed's expression was hopeful.

"I could."

Ross set the rest of the loaded sticks on the sand.

Delbert and Ross took hold of Jed and escorted him to their seats by the dying fire. Ross pointed to one remaining log and frowned. "That's it."

Delbert grunted. "That means we need to get more."

Ross stuck the log on the fire while Delbert gathered cones and small sticks and added them to the flames. The two boys went in search of more firewood.

They were quite a ways from camp when Delbert asked, "Did you bring the hatchet?"

"Nope. I thought you had it."

Delbert rolled his eyes. "You had it last. I'm not your ma. You can take care of it, too, ya know."

"It's your hatchet, Del."

"You had it last. Where is it?"

"I think I left it down by the creek."

"Great. We'll have to get dead scraps."

"I'll look over here." Ross veered right. "I'm not your ma," He mimicked.

"Didn't say you were." Delbert raised his voice.

"What a knot-head. How hard is it to pack the hatchet back to the fire? I'm tired of being his ma. He needs responsibility. Always the jokester." Delbert rambled until he discovered a dead tree in his path. He

176

broke off an armload of limbs and headed back to camp.

Ross caught up with him. He dragged a couple long, heavy limbs. "Is that all you have?"

"I found a huge tree back there. But for some odd reason I have no hatchet to hack it up with."

Delbert grunted.

They walked back to camp in silence.

At camp they stoked the fire. Time to check the traps.

Delbert admitted to himself that he was glad they ran out of wood. He didn't feel like telling another one of Pekam's stories.

They wandered to the traps, legs aching with fatigue. Delbert's gut fluttered. *Please let there be fish.*

Ross scratched his face. The urge overwhelmed him. As soon as he reached the bank, he scooped up water and shoved his face in his hands. He sighed and did it again.

Delbert watched him and tensed. He willed the fish to hold steady and not jump ship and swim away. "Can you create more of a commotion?"

"I can't help it. My skin's burnin'."

Delbert waded over to the first trap. A red bellied fish swam in circles. "I got one!" Ross jumped to his feet and ran to the other. "There's one in here!"

Jed hopped on his good leg and shouted, "We can eat. We have fish. Delbert did it." He toppled to the ground. "Delbert, we have food. You did it!" He grimaced as he rolled around in the sand.

"You all right?" Ross asked.

Jed nodded. "Ya, go check the other traps."

Delbert and Ross rushed to the other bank. "More

fish," Delbert shouted. They gathered the bounty in their shirts and headed to Jed.

Delbert stood taller, his steps longer.

At the fire, Delbert and Ross stuck fish on sticks and roasted them above tall flames. Delbert savored each bite. Sounds of delight resonated through camp.

Horse hooves could be heard in the distance.

Delbert rose and squinted. He made out a strong-looking male who sat tall in the saddle. *Could it be?*

"Who is it?" Jed craned his neck and wiped his fingers on his pants.

"*Wi, sintahoos.*" The man shouted while he waved one hand and held the reins of two horses in his other.

"Pekam!" Delbert raised both hands above his head. He waved a half-eaten fish on a stick in the air. He caught sight of someone on another horse who trailed behind Pekam. This man held the rein of a third horse. "Charlie!"

Pekam rode up and dismounted. Delbert recognized the other man as one of Pekam's cousins. The men unloaded a bundle of food and passed it out to the half-starved boys. "A gift from my sister."

Pekam focused on Ross. "Why is your face swollen?"

Ross blushed. "Wasps."

Pekam nodded. He and his cousin sat at the fire and listened to Delbert and the other two tell of their journey into manhood. It was a short one, since they were so eager to show off the weir.

Pekam's eyes glistened with pride as he studied the weir. He turned to Delbert. "I knew you didn't need me. Even when the horses showed up near the village. It was the Creator who trained you. He made you a warrior."

"We survived, didn't we?" Delbert said.

Pekam smiled. "You did. You and your weir."

They visited, caught up, and cooked more trout, before tearing down camp. Finally they loaded horses, lifted Jed onto his mount, and headed home.

ABOUT THE AUTHOR

Carmen Peone has lived in Northeast Washington and on the Colville Confederated Reservation since 1988. She had worked with Tribal Elder, Marguerite Ensminger, and other community elders and family learning the Arrow Lakes Language and various cultural traditions and legends. She lives with her husband who is a member of the Colville Confederated Tribes.

http://carmenpeone.com/